Jackie Tempo and the House of Wisdom

"*Jackie Tempo and the House of Wisdom* continues the adventures of an intrepid fifteen-year-old as she becomes personally involved with historical events. This delightful book is a pleasure to read, as the reader is catapulted back to a time and place that have become legendary.
Litrel is a gifted writer who makes this remote period sparkle with authentic detail. By incorporating the lesser-known history of the Abbasid dynasty, showing the Muslim emphasis on learning, explaining the role of Muslim women in this society, and how Greco-Roman thought was being preserved, Litrel breathes life into a world far removed from our own. Students and teachers of history alike will greatly enjoy this book."

Laurie Mannino
AP World History teacher, Montgomery County Public Schools, Maryland
College Board World History consultant
Advanced Placement World History exam reader/table leader

"Jackie Tempo is a teenage hero—clever, athletic, and resourceful. With the world literally spinning around her, she keeps her wits to save her family, her friends, and knowledge itself. The Jackie Tempo series is an engaging combination of adventure, time travel, and world history. *Jackie Tempo and the House of Wisdom* is a solid companion to Suzanne Litrel's earlier books, *Jackie Tempo and the Emperor's Seal* and *Jackie Tempo and the Ghost of Zumbi.*"
Patrick Whelan
Social Studies Department Head, Saint Stephen's Episcopal School, Bradenton, Florida
College Board World History consultant
Advanced Placement World History exam reader/table leader

* * *

Jackie Tempo and the Ghost of Zumbi (2009)

"Suzanne Litrel IS Jackie Tempo. Litrel's adolescent travel experiences, backed by a vast world history teaching background, produce a valuable and exciting motivation for young readers to think about history. Storytelling and historical fiction blend in *Jackie Tempo and the Ghost of Zumbi* to do just that—excite young readers to enjoy history."

John Maunu
College Board World History consultant, AP World History reader/table leader
2002–2003 Michigan Education Association Global and Diversity Educator of the Year

* * *

"*Jackie Tempo and the Ghost of Zumbi* is a fast-paced and fun-filled adventure that both entertains and educates. ... [H]istorical information, integral to understanding both the characters and the context of the time, [is] seamlessly incorporated throughout the story line. It is rich in detail with engaging characters, multiple story lines, and a plot with more than enough twists to keep the reader in suspense. I highly recommend *Jackie Tempo and the Ghost of Zumbi* for teens, parents, and teachers alike."

Linda Black, PhD
Secondary Education Department, Stephen F. Austin State University

* * *

"*The Ghost of Zumbi*—and the basic premise of the Jackie Tempo series—allows young readers to travel through world history with a sympathetic, daring character of their own age.

These stories are a boon to teachers of world history, helping them get students imaginatively engaged in the essential themes and processes of the discipline."

Ryba L. Epstein
Advanced Placement instructor
College Board World History consultant (Chicago)

Jackie Tempo and the Emperor's Seal (2007)

"A history assignment leads to a fantasy infused with a mélange of Chinese philosophy and modern-day deception. ... Litrel's descriptive scenes of the crowded, loud, exotic, dangerous world of medieval China provide an authentic flavor to the story's background."
Kirkus Discoveries

* * *

"The story ... is an enjoyable way to grasp [traditional Chinese] concepts of filial piety, the role of women, governmental administration, and family relationships. ... The love of reading, the importance of books, and the love of knowledge was deftly managed in the story."
Gloria Sesso, director of social studies, Patchogue-Medford Schools
co-president, Long Island Council for Social Studies

**Please visit www.jackietempo.com
for more on the Jackie Tempo series and for discussion
guides to each book.**

Jackie Tempo
and the
House of Wisdom

Suzanne Litrel

iUniverse, Inc.
Bloomington

Jackie Tempo and the House of Wisdom

iUniverse books may be ordered through booksellers or by contacting:

iUniverse
1663 Liberty Drive
Bloomington, IN 47403
www.iuniverse.com
1-800-Authors (1-800-288-4677)

ISBN: 978-1-4620-5886-0 (sc)
ISBN: 978-1-4620-5887-7 (hc)
ISBN: 978-1-4759-0804-6 (e)

Library of Congress Control Number: 2012937135

Printed in the United States of America
iUniverse rev. date: 05/07/2012

Also by Suzanne Litrel

Fiction
Jackie Tempo and the Emperor's Seal
Jackie Tempo and the Ghost of Zumbi

Nonfiction
Contributing author, *Teaching World History in the 21st Century*
(Heidi Roupp, editor)

This book is dedicated to the memory of my father,
Sandro Domenico Segalini.
He always sought the Truth.

Acknowledgments

THIS BOOK WOULD HAVE LANGUISHED in my files—and in my head—had it not been for my friends and family pushing me to get off my duff and get down to business. My AP World History colleagues, in particular, have been quite insistent. "I'm working on it" was my excuse to Ryba Epstein. "That's what you said last year," she retorted. Pat Whelan got on my case to get the book out by the holidays, and John Maunu reminded me that his granddaughter was going through the series, and what about the next book? Thanks also to my "big sister" Laurie Maninno, and to countless others for their constant encouragement and support.

Thanks also go to my brilliant, hardworking, and unrelenting editor Karen Schader, who let me get away with absolutely nothing! Her keen eye kept this story on track. In addition, the iUniverse team deserves much acknowledgment for their hard work.

My sisters Debbie Kloosterman and Carolyn Segalini have served as cheerleaders throughout, and their unflagging enthusiasm has helped spur me to action.

My children were, as usual, tolerant and supportive during the summer this book came to fruition. This was also true of my husband, Christopher, who always makes things "go right."

Seek ye knowledge, even unto China.
—Mohammed, Prophet of Islam

Chapter I

Flight

Baghdad, 927 CE

"Allahu Akbar!" As the last prayers of the evening died away, a young man rolled up his prayer mat, adjusted his turban, and stole across the great courtyard. He glanced nervously up at the two-story building that ringed the open space, housing students above and vast libraries below.

There it was again—a quick flash, a shimmer of movement from one of the many arched portals of the Bayt al-Hikma, Baghdad's newly constructed House of Wisdom. He was being watched, of that he had no doubt. He forced his attention on what lay before him—the vast space he had yet to traverse. But under the dark, yawning sky made bright by a thousand and one stars, the young scholar felt as insignificant as a grain of sand in the wide, rolling Sahara. He took a deep breath and pushed through an intense crowd, students and teachers connected by their love of learning.

There, in the intellectual center of the Islamic world, the most brilliant of scholars resumed their heated debates, begun long before the call to prayer. He made his way through the clusters of arguing men, moving quickly, but mindful of his step. Currents of conversation eddied around him, luring him with the same siren song: the pursuit of Truth.

"According to Aristotle's discourse on the nature of politics, there …"

"Pah! You can do better work than that!"

"You doubt my abilities as translator? I will show you his words myself!"

"Come, come, peace be with you, my friends, the hour is late. Tomorrow we will examine the document together, for three minds are greater than one, *neh*?"

"Agreed. That you have delved so deeply into the lost wisdom of the ancients is impressive. No doubt the quality of the manuscript has suffered much in its long journey from Byzantium. I apologize for my harsh words."

And from another group: "But the Ptolemaic view is not rational. Here, let us examine this from a strictly mathematical perspective."

"Yes, yes, let us not forget that mathematics is the foundation of all science."

The moon shone down in full on the open space, bathing the scholars in a clear, pure light. The young man had almost reached the far end of the courtyard when he slowed to mop the perspiration from his brow, well aware of the small but forbidden document he had tucked into his turban hours earlier. He should never have stopped for such a trivial task as wiping his forehead. A thin hand snaked out and snared the sleeve of his scholar's robe.

A bemused voice followed the hand. "Where do you think you're going, my friend?" Dark eyes peered from beneath blindingly white, bushy brows. "I'm surprised you're not interested in chatting about Galen's classification"—still clutching the young man tightly—"over there." Gnarled with age, the ropy hand lifted slowly and pointed to a group of three young men.

They were dark and earnest, and much like the trapped scholar, made all the more appealing by their obvious intellect. One leaned forward in serious debate, traditional side curls swinging as he made his point.

Suddenly, another gave a great shout and a laugh, clapping the Jewish scholar on the back. "Ah, my friends, we are all People of the Book, which is why we agree on that which is truly important!" exclaimed their Muslim peer, pushing back his turban with a wide smile.

"Truth!" exclaimed the third, touching the simple cross embroidered on his tunic. And all nodded in agreement.

The three young scholars disappeared into the shadows of the great courtyard, laughing softly as Muslims, Christians, and Jews made their way home for the night.

"Ah … to pursue Truth: that is what we do here, in Baghdad's wondrous House of Wisdom," said the old man. "Indeed, this great era, praise Allah, is unrivaled in the history of scholarship!" He fixed a stony gaze on the young scholar, still frozen in his tracks.

Now the old man drew closer, and the movement made his turban slip slightly. "Truth," he hissed, "is revealed only to those who are most worthy."

The younger man nodded and stumbled back.

"And never forget it."

The scholar nodded once more, mute. It would be impossible to do otherwise.

The knowledge of anything, since all things have causes,
is not acquired or complete unless it is known by its causes.
—Ibn Sina

Chapter II

Houses of Wisdom

Arborville High School, present time

"OKAY, LET'S GET STARTED." AT their teacher's command, the tenth-grade students pushed back from their tables of four and began to move about the vast library, intent on beginning their research. Only Jackie Tempo lingered in her seat, tilting her head; her eyes swept over the elaborate tin ceiling, which was supported by eight twenty-foot-high Doric columns. These massive posts with smooth, round caps that grazed the ceiling were symmetrically arranged down the length of the library, four on each side.

"Wow, what a place," she mused half aloud, pushing a tousled lock of auburn hair aside for a better view.

"Our library is indeed quite impressive." The school librarian smiled down at her, arms full of books on Islamic art and architecture. Mrs. Housel was a tiny woman, not much taller than Jackie when the girl was sitting down.

"The transformation has been remarkable," said Mrs. Housel, reflecting on the endowment that had created the dazzling space.

Arborville High School had been given five million dollars by Dr. Gordon Knotte, class of '68; most of the money was earmarked for the library's renovation. The only stipulation was that the building contractors follow the exact set of drawings provided by the donor's architect.

"And to think I graduated in the same class as Gordon Knotte," Mrs. Housel mused. "No one predicted what he would accomplish one day."

It was certainly not hard to imagine the millions poured into the library: mahogany stacks reached toward the ceiling, and light streamed in from a beautiful stained-glass window in the center of the space, creating a shimmering kaleidoscope of colors on the creamy marble floor. *Like a cathedral*, Jackie thought. *A holy place.*

"What was he like?" she asked Mrs. Housel. "Why did he put all this money into the library?"

As she spoke, Jackie realized that Anthony Milano, her research partner, was waving her over furiously. "C'mon!" he mouthed silently, standing next to a computer. But Jackie didn't feel like starting her work just yet. She did her best to ignore him.

"Well," Mrs. Housel began, "no one really knew him very well—except perhaps me, as we both spent so much time here— that is, in the old library. He would come in searching for the oddest books—never any pattern to them, except that they were all academic, and rarely fiction. Science, literature, history, philosophy—he was an avid reader in all subjects. I never imagined that he'd put his learning to such fantastic use."

That he had. Mrs. Housel explained that although Gordon Knotte had become a renowned inventor and physicist, he had really made his fortune in the business world. A reclusive billionaire, he invested in companies he believed in and would give struggling businesses a chance in return for a healthy chunk of ownership. He lived simply, never married, and gave away most of his profits to worthy causes. Like this library.

Mrs. Housel recalled Knotte's words to the school board the day he quietly handed over a stunningly generous check for renovations. "Gordon said it was in this library that he first understood that the borders of Arborville—indeed of the world—existed only in his mind. He was right." She smiled at Jackie. "I remember he said something about building a 'palace of learning.' I think he accomplished his goal."

Jackie smiled in agreement. "Where is he now?" she asked the librarian.

Mrs. Housel gave a dismissive shrug, her tiny shoulders lifting her rose-colored cardigan a fraction of an inch. "I really have no idea," she said, and moved on to help another student. Jackie stared after her in thought. The librarian was rarely so abrupt.

"Uh, can we finish this project before we graduate from high school?" Anthony asked mildly, sauntering over. But Jackie could tell that he was irritated at having been kept waiting. "I can make myself useful someplace else, if you know what I mean." He winked at a pretty blonde at another table, and then he brushed an imaginary piece of lint off his shoulder as he gave the library a suspicious once-over. He made a show of hating all books. "I'm allergic to the written word," he had once proclaimed to Jackie, who had long since given up trying to convince him otherwise.

Jackie rolled her eyes at her friend. In the few months since she'd come to live with her aunt Isobel and started at Arborville High School, she had learned that Anthony Milano appeared to be far more interested in fashion—and women—than anything else. The only reading he ever did publicly in school, when he should have been busy with assigned work, consisted of short articles from magazines with headings like "Dress to Impress" and "Casual, but Cool." But he was also fiercely intelligent and deeply loyal—and most important, he didn't bug Jackie with too many questions about her past. In return, she played along with his supposed shallowness, as she knew his neighborhood friends gave him enough grief for being in advanced classes. In this way, they covered for each other.

Jackie grinned at him now. "All right, Casanova"—she hooked her arm in his—"let's head over to the computers first."

Anthony sighed irritably. "I was just over there!" He shrugged. "Typical female—don't know your own mind."

"Hey!" Jackie gave him a playful punch as they made their way down to the vast row of computers. Anthony laughed and threw up his hands in mock defeat.

Jackie felt a warm hand on her shoulder. A deep voice said, "Hey yourself—and you, don't pick on my old pal!"

She knew that voice. She spun around, blushing, long red hair whipping across her face.

"I didn't touch her, I swear!" Anthony grinned at Jon Durrie, his childhood friend and neighbor. They had both come from difficult circumstances, having grown up on the "wrong side of the tracks"; theirs was a friendship born of tough situations, and the result was a bond that was hard to break.

"You're a lucky man, Durrie, if you get what I mean," Anthony said, and winked broadly.

Mortified, Jackie closed her eyes and wished herself away from the scene. Her face was so hot, she thought she'd self-combust.

"Out—get out," the tall, athletic senior ordered Anthony. "Go do some work. Your teacher's watching you." It was true. Ms. Thompson, the tenth-graders' history teacher, had taken a threatening step toward Anthony, her lovely features creased in a frown.

"What about you?" Anthony retorted. Then he sat down at a computer station, carefully folding his jacket over the back of his mahogany chair. "Oh yeah, I forgot. You're her favorite."

"Yes I am." Jon grinned and waved at Ms. Thompson, who gave him a puzzled smile and waved back.

Jackie almost laughed out loud—it was amazing how clueless teachers really were. Just a few days ago, Ms. Thompson had drawn her aside to issue a warning about Anthony. "Watch out for Romeo there," she'd said. "He's very smart, but lazy, and he'll dump you the first chance he gets."

Jackie had nearly choked on stifled laughter, and her young history teacher mistook her reaction for distress. "Sorry, sorry, didn't mean to pry." Flustered, she had handed Jackie an entire tissue box and walked away.

Ms. Thompson had been way off target; Jackie was not at all romantically involved with Anthony. In fact, she and Jon had started seeing more of each other in the last three weeks, ever since Jon's mother's cancer had gone into remission. The cross-country season was over, and they both had more time on their hands now that they weren't training several hours a day. They had been to the movies twice and out walking around town, quiet now that tourist season was over and the cold had started to set in.

"So what are you guys working on?" Jon steered her to the library stacks, his hand firmly on the small of her back. He had no class this period and was in the library looking for a good book to read. He always insisted that leaving the school was a waste of time—if he went out for food, he'd lose his parking space. Of course, he'd never admit that a pretty redhead was the real reason he hung around campus.

Jackie slouched against a section of books, smiling up at the handsome senior.

"Well?" Jon leaned over her, pushing aside his dark hair; his blue eyes bored into her own. Jackie started, and she accidentally elbowed a thick text out the other side. It made a *thunk* as it hit the dense floor. She ducked under Jon's arm and ran around the stack to retrieve it.

"Um … this, actually." Jackie was stunned to realize she'd found the very book she needed for her project, one that had been checked out for weeks now. She glanced up at the sequencing of books. It had clearly been misshelved. Jon had followed her around the stack, and reached for the book.

"*Architectural Mysteries of the Abbasid Era,*" he read aloud. "Interesting take on the Golden Age of Islam."

"Is there anything you don't know?" Jackie pushed him out toward the table where she and Anthony had all their stuff.

"Oh, c'mon, that's pretty basic," Jon shot back. "You know, advances in math and science, thanks to a major translation push during the reign of Caliph al-Ma'mun, who—"

"—had sent scholars to Byzantium to retrieve ancient Greek documents, which the emperor had no use for anyway, and then the scholars from the House of Baghdad set about translating Aristotle's works, for example." Jackie smiled and leafed casually through the book. "Nerd."

"You're both lost causes." Anthony joined them at the table. "Okay, so I found this really cool site that claims the House of Wisdom was a cover-up for something else." He pushed up the sleeves of his Abercrombie shirt.

Jon looked at him, amused, and clasped his hands on the table. "Anthony, how can I take a fashionista like you seriously?"

Anthony sighed and pulled a comb out of his back pocket, slicking back his jet-black hair. "You're just jealous. Know how much this shirt is worth?"

Jon shrugged.

"About a buck fifty." Anthony grinned and leaned back in his chair, clearly proud of himself.

"Yeah, a dollar fifty sounds right—what is that, polyester?" Jon said. Jackie kicked him under the table.

"Very funny, moh-ron, one hundred and fifty dollars. That's right," said Anthony, noting their shocked looks with satisfaction. "But I got a deal on it … ten buckaroos!"

Jon laughed at Anthony's expression of vanity and thriftiness. "Typical!" The bell rang.

"Style, my friends, I got it—stick around and you might learn something." Anthony sauntered off, leaving them with a mess of books on the table.

"Jon, go. You'll be late for class." Jackie tried to shoo him away. "I have lunch—and anyway, I'm going to stay and look through these books a bit. I'm not hungry yet."

Jon raised a brow at the waifish redhead. "You shouldn't skip lunch," he said with a touch of concern. "Promise me you won't."

Already deep in a thick volume about Islamic culture during the Abbasid dynasty, Jackie smiled absentmindedly, transfixed by the rich images before her. "Yeah, sure," she said, leafing through the pages. It was true that there were days when she was far more interested in reading than eating, and so far this seemed to be one of them. "Dona Marta packed my lunch, and I can eat it in health class. Ten thirty in the morning is way too early to eat a tuna sandwich."

"You still need to eat," Jon insisted.

"Mm-hmm," Jackie replied, her long locks tumbling over an image of one of the many minarets in Baghdad.

Jon sighed, leaned over, and kissed the top of her head. "See you after school." She ducked her head, smiling deeply, and reached for another book as he walked away.

Then she turned to the page before her.

* * *

Baghdad, 927 CE

The young scholar unwrapped his turban and set it down on his sleeping pallet. Even now, in the safety of his room, his fingers trembled. He pulled a thin strip of writing from within the folds of the soft cloth.

"*The Sultan's Secret*," he whispered anxiously to himself. Of course he was troubled. By removing a portion of a document from the House of Wisdom, he had committed a serious crime, punishable by death.

Still, he had no choice. Several years ago, three powerful books had vanished from his father's library in Samarkand. It was certain that they would fetch a high price in a world that treasured books and learning; indeed, the caliph had funded costly expeditions in search of far less than what these books contained. The young man, fondly known as Shahan to his family and friends, had reasoned that the texts would most likely turn up in Baghdad's House of Wisdom, and against his father's wishes, had set out to recover the stolen books.

"The books are a holy terror," his father had argued. "Seek them, and be destroyed!"

Shahan was resolute. "And should I stay, the results might be the same—for all of us."

In the years that followed, Shahan had immersed himself in learning, even as he sought the stolen texts. His academic credentials had gained him easy access to the archives, and his intellectual ability was evident for all to see. He had made himself useful at once, translating and interpreting ancient documents from Byzantium. Time passed quickly.

Until today. He had stumbled upon a document that referred to the stolen books. It also mentioned a strange interpretation of the universe—and its infinite possibilities. The irony of his actions was not lost on Shahan as he slid the document into his robes and later, put the piece in his turban. He needed time—alone—to properly interpret the text.

But this was not the work of a scholar; this was not even an ancient document, he thought with defiance. This was … pure and unimaginable evil. He could hardly believe his eyes as he stared at the inscriptions and formulas. "May Allah forgive the person who wrote this," he said aloud. But the earnest young man was transfixed. He read on. He moved his oil lamp closer, fully intending to burn the writing when he was finished.

He would have no such opportunity this night. A heavy hand swung through the air and slammed into his temple. The scholar crumpled noiselessly to the floor.

"Better you should pray for your life, my young friend." The intruder's hairy hand snatched up the writing. "Such a secret should be entrusted only to those who are worthy—as am I." Then the lamp went out, and the room was black as pitch.

Intentions count in your actions.
—Abu Bakr

Chapter III

Found

Arborville High School, present time

TIME SEEMED TO LOSE ALL meaning in the serene high school library. Jackie tucked her feet under her and leaned hard on her elbows on the shiny mahogany table, drinking in the dazzling images and descriptions in the oversized book that was open before her.

> *All throughout Dar al-Islam, libraries and universities flourished in the medieval era, even as western Europeans languished in the stupor that set in after the fall of Rome.*

As she leafed through the book, Jackie was confronted with dazzling images of mosques and minarets, and learned men deep in thought, poring over texts. She stared at a calligraphy piece. The Arabic script was elegant and firm; it seemed to reach to the very heavens in supplication, searching for answers to universal truths. Not for the first time, Jackie wished she could read Arabic.

"Seek ye knowledge, even unto China."

Jackie sat upright at the strange whisper that echoed through the cavernous room, but the library had emptied out, and Mrs. Housel was nowhere in sight. She squinted, straining her eyes to see down the length of the library. With a shiver, she tucked an errant red lock behind her ear. Nothing. The marble floors gleamed quietly under the warm, bright ceiling lights.

Had she imagined the voice? *Just a bit more,* she told herself. Then she'd go to lunch. She would just do a quick search on Baghdad's House of Wisdom, and she got up to use the library's electronic catalog. *Hurry, hurry,* she urged silently, willing the computer to speed up the search. She typed in "House of Wisdom": nothing. Next, she typed in "Abbasid dynasty": this time, too broad. Not for the first time, she was irritated that she couldn't do all her research online. She needed at least two book sources, or she and Anthony would get no credit for their project.

Mrs. Housel still hadn't returned; the hairs on the back of Jackie's neck stood up, and goose bumps covered her arms. But stubbornness stayed her fear—she was determined to check out a book now. She tapped her foot, antsy and impatient.

"Baghdad, medieval era"

Tap, tap, tap. Not found.

"Harun al-Rashid, caliph and founder of the House of Wisdom"

Tap, tap, tap. Not found.

"Baghdad, achievements"

Tap, tap, tap. Not found.

"Islam—cultural achievements"

Twenty-five entries. Jackie's foot slowed as she scanned them all and stopped altogether when she came to "Preservation of Greco-Roman Culture," with three entries. She jotted them all down and went to the stacks to retrieve the books.

As she was loading the last book into her arms, she heard the voice again, this time a bit more loudly.

"The ink of a scholar ... is worth more than the blood of a martyr."

She stepped out of the stacks and looked around. Mrs. Housel was returning to her desk, a mere speck all the way down the length of the grand library. Jackie almost shouted with relief.

"Mohammed says …" The voice was louder, more insistent now.

Choking back her fear, she moved nearer to the source. It seemed to be coming from the next stack over. *Well, I've faced worse,* she thought, and then swung around to confront the noise.

"Mankind is not without …"

"Oh!" No one was there. Something was amiss. Jackie stepped slowly into the stacks; a lone book was jutting out an inch. She knelt and pulled it out.

"*Infinite Knowledge, Eternal Life,*" she read the first part of the title aloud, and shivered. Then she whispered the subtitle: "*The House of Wisdom.*"

It was just the book she was looking for.

The ink of a scholar is worth more than the blood of a martyr.
—Mohammed, prophet of Islam

Chapter IV

True Devotion

Baghdad, 927 CE

"SHAHAN WAS NOT AT EARLY-MORNING prayers." A middle-aged scholar bent over the work in front of him, his lips barely moving as he relayed the news.

"So?" came the library director's retort. "We have much work to do, Achmed; it is not our concern." The director was an elderly gentleman who spent much of the time on his own research. He now pushed back the voluminous sleeves of his robes and snorted impatiently. "Allah willing, I might be able to finish this translation—if I'm left in peace."

Achmed leaned across the wide-planked wooden desk they were sharing in the library. "Mohammed, most revered director, I am humbled to call you my friend. But what in the name of the Rightly Guided Caliphs is so very difficult that you cannot carry on a discourse and complete your translations at the same time?"

The elderly scholar reached under his turban to scratch his head. Ten in the morning, and already all of Baghdad was sweltering under brutal heat. He sighed.

"Euclid and his theory of angles." Mohammed put a hand to his pounding head. "The translation of his *Elements* was excellent, the greatest treasure given to Caliph Harun al-Ma'mun so many years before." He sighed. "I understand his ideas, even if we do not have a vocabulary for them and thus cannot proceed with a direct translation. So it is that we must be very careful in moving forward with the interpretation of his work."

Achmed nodded. It was true. Al-Mansur, the founder of Baghdad, had proclaimed that the city was a "gift of God." As such, it would be the intellectual seat of the Abbasid dynasty. Later, the caliph Harun al-Ma'mun had ordered the procurement of Greek documents from Byzantium and had them transported all the way to Baghdad; it was here that the finest minds of Dar al-Islam, the House of Islam, had set upon deciphering the work. This was known as the Translation Movement. However, not only translation was required of the intellectuals: the creation of a whole new vocabulary was needed as well, as they sought to grasp the academic advances of the ancient world. It was this task that they had struggled with for weeks and months—even years.

"Ah, those Greek mathematicians." Achmed nodded, patting his nose, a quirky habit he'd had since his early days at the neighborhood madrassa, the school where he learned the fundamentals of Islamic thought, as well as how to read and write in Arabic. "Some of their work is very different indeed."

"But much of it is true," said old Mohammed, frowning. He rubbed his brow as if he could wipe away the frown altogether. "The Greeks and their advanced knowledge of astronomy—very important, of course, so that proper respect to Allah can be given."

"Yes," said Achmed, "every true believer must know the way to Mecca."

Mohammed nodded and wished for a cup of tea, despite the blazing heat. "I was fortunate enough to make the journey not once, but thrice in my lifetime."

"Praise be to Allah! You are most devoted." Achmed's effusive manner hid his own guilt at never having been able to complete this act of devotion required of all able-bodied Muslims. But the time had not yet come. He was so close, so close to uncovering the greatest academic discovery of all time, that which so many had sought through the ages … and if he left now, the chance to truly pay homage to Allah might be lost—forever. He dabbed at his brow. Then he beckoned impatiently to one of the figures waiting in the corner.

A young slave in a simple tunic stepped forward. "Yes, master?" He was no more than twelve, yet he was quick of mind and fleet of foot. Achmed had heard that he was a son of a warrior king from a village of unbelievers in the great African empire of Ghana.

Achmed had a simple request: "Please bring me some paper."

The boy's eyes widened at the thought of handling the stuff. He had never touched it before, but he could see that it was delicate and of great use to the scholars here. He gave a slight nod, and withdrew to fulfill the task.

"The find of a century," Achmed said to Mohammed, who was frowning over a group of triangles.

"Yes, a good battle always yields such treasure." Mohammed looked up with a wry smile. "Since the Battle of Talas, when we … ah … extracted the art of papermaking from Chinese prisoners of war, we have made ample use of paper. Allah willed that this knowledge should come to us; clearly, the faithful are most deserving."

The slave boy returned with a few whispery pages, just in time to catch the last part of the sentence. It did seem that the scholars put their writing to good use. To his young mind, those who sat at the tables the longest were the most revered, and in fact, the boy had started to study the strange scratches on the documents as well. He was fascinated by the drawings and the symbols that were supposed to be words.

The boy had come to learn that the library director held the most exalted position in the House of Wisdom; he was also a scholar in his own right, who worked beside and among the other men here. Patrons were also quite important, and some had even donated their own personal libraries to the building, so that others might peruse them.

Achmed was one such person, and that meant he was never to be denied when he made a request. Like now. The boy handed over the paper he had carefully retrieved, and when Achmed pressed a small note into his hand, he knew better than to betray the exchange. Later, as Achmed had taught him, he would pass the message on to the one who always waited, quiet and still, in an unmarked alley just north of this famous center of learning.

"Go now and complete your errand." Achmed and the slave boy knew he was referring to the note that was exchanged between them.

The boy nodded. He was extraordinarily bright, and handsome as well; his dark almond-shaped eyes curved up ever so slightly over high, sculpted cheekbones. Although he was a slave, it was possible that by making himself useful to the library staff and patrons, he could gain freedoms, some of which could be considerable. The boy was just beginning to grasp this.

"And if you would also—"

"*Ey!*" The boy stepped back and pointed.

Mohammed had slumped over the table, spittle flecking the corners of his mouth. His arms hung by his side, slack. His eyes had closed, and he didn't seem to be breathing.   Achmed impatiently motioned to the boy, who had paled at the sight of the inert old man. "Get him off these writings!" As much as Achmed admired old Mohammed, the man was endangering the works of the ancient Greek mathematician Euclid. As director, he should have known better. This would never do.

Chairs scraped backward, a grating sound against the cool tiled floor. A half-dozen pairs of hands swooped to the rescue as translators, scribes, and scholars at the next table rushed to help.

It was too late.

A hush. Then: "Mohammed is dead."

*The world is divided into men who have wit and no religion
and men who have religion and no wit.*
—Ibn Sina

Chapter V

The Real Challenge

Arborville High School, present day

"If you believe in Mohammed, Mohammed is dead …"

Jackie frowned as she read the words aloud. Three heads bent over the quote in the document packet on Islam. The sophomores had less than a minute to decipher the words and share their ideas with the class. Unbeknownst to their world history teacher, Anthony was trying to text his latest conquest, so technically only Jackie and Samantha Jackson had actually glanced at the words—and Sam was distracted. Her fencing team was going head-to-head against the state champions right after school.

"Sorry," Samantha said, shaking her head. "I can't think straight. I'm nervous about today's fencing bout. And the blade of my favorite saber broke off in yesterday's practice." She took a deep breath.

"Niiice!" Anthony looked up from his cell phone and grinned at the discussion. "Any blood? I like to watch chicks fight!"

"Shut up, Anthony," Jackie said. "She's nervous enough—this is only the team's second year."

"Yeah—I still don't know half of what I need to defend against the Oakdale team." The captain of the saber squad bit her nails. "Losing is bad enough, but those girls are evil. They're rich, spoiled, and mean. And we're going to be slaughtered," she moaned.

Now Sam clutched her pen—hard. Her knuckles turned white as she attempted to underline key words in the document packet.

Jackie finished reading the quote from Abu Bakr, the first of the so-called Rightly Guided Caliphs of the early Islamic world: "… but if you believe in Allah, then Allah is alive." She looked up. "What do you think, Sam? Propaganda? Or did he really mean that God—Allah—is eternal?" She ignored Anthony, who looked puzzled as he slid his cell phone into his back pocket.

"Anthony Giovanni Milano!" Ms. Thompson invoked his name in perfect Florentine Italian. She was at his shoulder, one hand on her hip, the other palm out, waiting. "Hand it over. Now!" She spoke quietly, so as not to disrupt the entire class, but the menace in her voice was quite real.

Anthony winced. "Aw, Ms. Thompson, I—"

The elegant young teacher took a sharp breath and widened her eyes, shocked that he didn't give her the cell phone right away. He sighed and put it in her palm.

"Tell your mother she can pick it up when she meets with me." Ms. Thompson strode off. "Let's turn our chairs around, class. Get ready to discuss your documents."

"Damn, there go all my contacts," Anthony muttered.

Sam snorted, but Jackie noticed that he was paler than usual.

"What is it?" she whispered as she turned her chair to face the front of the room. Ms. Thompson had the chairs in semicircles, and Jackie liked that she had a seat at the center of the class, so she could focus on the lessons better. Anthony, on the other hand, was always getting in trouble.

"Just some angry ex," he said distractedly, reaching into his backpack for a pen. "Another lost opportunity."

"You'll get it back," Jackie wrote on his notebook. She was referring to the cell phone, not the girl. He shot her a look of despair and shook his head.

Jackie was surprised—not much rattled her friend. "Are you sure that's all?" she wrote. Ms. Thompson's voice, a shade louder than usual, cut right into her thoughts.

"All right, then, Jackie's group wants to share their findings with the class." Jackie swallowed hard. She liked Ms. Thompson and didn't want her to be angry with them. She looked at Samantha, who nodded.

"Well," Jackie began, leaning forward in her chair, "we're on document one, a quote attributed to Abu Bakr, Mohammed's uncle." Ms. Thompson nodded encouragingly.

Jackie continued. "Basically, he said, 'If you believe in Mohammed, then Mohammed is dead. But if you believe in Allah, then Allah lives on forever.' He said those words right after Mohammed's death in 632 CE, in the Common Era. He knew that the Bedouin tribes of the Arabian Peninsula had a shaky truce while Mohammed was alive, and he had wanted to keep the peace so that Islam could flourish and expand."

"What do you mean, truce?" The comment sounded innocent enough, but Jackie knew that it was meant to be snarky. Vivienne Marche, currently number one in their sophomore class, constantly challenged her every word; she was quite upset that Jackie had scored the highest grade on the last exam, and had been trying to discredit her in class ever since the grades had come out. "Everyone knows that Arabs can never get along. And anyway, Muslims are all about jihad—you know, fighting."

Jackie tensed. She realized that Vivienne was trying to bait her. She stared at Vivienne's lime-green Coach bag, occupying a most conspicuous position on her desk. She remembered how she had overheard the tall, thin blonde say that the two-hundred-dollar purse was a gift for being number one in the class.

Clearly, Vivienne was after more gifts. She crossed her Ugg-booted legs as well as her arms and glared at her auburn-haired opponent. Jackie stifled a smile; the girl looked like a pretzel. She had just opened her mouth to respond when Anthony cut in.

"Ah, c'mon, you gotta know the deal about jihad—sheesh!" Anthony casually slung his arm around the back of Jackie's chair.

She smiled to herself; his gesture told her that he was bracing to do battle with Vivienne. She sat up, interested in what would come next.

"What do you mean, Anthony?" Ms. Thompson raised a brow.

"Well, jihad refers to struggle—right?—and in particular, the struggle for faith. That is, what the Muslims called true faith. Beginning with the belief in one god and only one god—Allah. So sometimes jihad was manifested by war, but at other times, it referred to one's inner struggle to stay true to Allah. That was the real challenge," Anthony explained in earnest, and then caught himself. "If you know what I mean."

He looked around, slightly embarrassed, caught Sam's eye, and winked. "Like our fencing captain's going to do battle this afternoon and—"

Sam rolled her eyes.

Ms. Thompson broke in. "Very impressive, Anthony, and let's stay on topic, shall we?" It was clear that the teacher was, in fact, pleased with Anthony's rebuttal. "Now let's use our documents to address the issue at hand: to what extent did Muslim culture support an environment of learning and discovery? Then we'll compare Dar al-Islam—the Muslim world, or House of Islam—to other regional civilizations, like China and Western Europe."

Anthony's hand shot up again: "During the Umayyad or Abbasid era?" Vivienne gave him a dirty look, and he secretly flipped her the finger. Jackie suppressed a giggle. Clearly, this was turning out to be an interesting day.

As the conversation wore on, Jackie's gaze wandered over the numerous posters adorning Ms. Thompson's room. She had filled nearly every free bit of wall space, and even the ceiling, with posters from times past, as well as famous quotes from great historical figures.

"Be the change you want to see in the world": Jackie read Mahatma Gandhi's words for the millionth time. Her eyes traveled over a cluster of posters depicting famous philosophers engaging in discussion. There was Socrates, debating with Xenophon; at their feet was Averroes, leaning over Pythagoras's shoulder; and at the center of the famous piece, Plato held forth with his student Aristotle. Then there was copy of a Persian miniature of Caliph al-Ma'mun, perhaps the most learned caliph of the Abbasid dynasty, sitting up in his bed and conversing with Aristotle. It had been said that this dream conversation between Muslim ruler and ancient Greek philosopher was what had prompted him to build the House of Wisdom in the first place. "What's the connection?" read the heading to this bulletin board. "Does real learning take place in isolation, or is it part of a larger continuum?"

Jackie sighed. Her parents would have loved this class. College professors, they'd be pleased to find that she was challenged on a daily basis in world history. Even better, Ms. Thompson always found a way to connect their learning to lessons they could apply today. If only they could meet Ms. Thompson ...

She started to doodle, thinking about the events of the last few weeks and what she'd discovered about her parents. That they had not, in fact, been killed in a car accident, leaving Aunt Isobel as her own family, as she had initially believed. That the two history professors were traveling together across time and space. That Devon Pearson, her father's grad student, had acquired the ability to make quantum leaps across time, and was doing so for his own gain, despite the family fortune he stood to inherit. That her parents were hunting him down, fearful that he might cause a major disruption to the time-space continuum. And that three books from ancient Samarkand had given them all the ability to make time bend. Jackie's parents had one, Devon had stolen another, and Jackie had the third, hidden in her aunt Isobel's library.

She stared at the designs she'd scrawled on her battered notebook: swirling, mysterious, seemingly without end. How on earth had it come to this? Her parents were destined to be lost in another place, desperate to find Devon, lest he misuse the power of the book.

Jackie sighed, twirling a long lock of curly red hair around her finger, and began filling in the rest of the space on the page. As she drew, the outside world seemed to ebb, and she became lost in the design. She, too, had traveled across time to find her parents, but the reality was that they were on a journey of their own. Her chest ached with loneliness and fear; they would have to find their own way back, in their own time. Then she thought of Jon, the only person she could really talk to about this.

Once he had been just her history tutor. When she had first come to stay with Aunt Isobel, Jackie was too depressed to think clearly, so Jon had been hired to help with her studies. Now the captain of the cross-country team was her very, very close friend. Jon had actually had the misfortune (as he put it) of traveling back in time with her to sixteenth-century China, so he well understood Jackie's situation. All that time together had changed the nature of their relationship, and though the cross-country season had ended, they were spending more and more time together. They both knew their friendship was evolving into something more, and she smiled at the thought of it.

"Here's an example of an arabesque," said Ms. Thompson with a grin, holding Jackie's well-adorned notebook in the air. "Who can tell me why?" Jackie covered her eyes, mortified.

"At least you didn't write 'I heart Jon' all over it," Anthony whispered, but loud enough for their side of the room to hear. Jackie elbowed him in the ribs.

Vivienne raised her hand and gave Jackie and Anthony a malicious look. Sam quickly raised her hand, too, and Ms. Thompson picked on her to speak. Jackie knew how Sam felt about speaking up in class, and threw her a grateful glance.

"Well, doesn't *arabesque* mean a repetitive pattern? You know, like—"

"Fire drill!" one of the students shouted from the hallway. In fact, the alarm had been sounded—a horrible, jarring, continual ringing—and blue emergency lights in the hallway started to flash on and off.

"I don't think it's a drill," said Ms. Thompson, quickly gathering up her keys. "Out, everyone, out!" Her voice carried above the din. "Now!" The students dropped their belongings and filed quickly and silently out the door.

Within minutes, the entire building had emptied, and school guards talked in hushed tones as they swept the area. Despite the brightness of the day, students and teachers shivered in the early December wind. They were quiet, preserving all their energy to stay warm, and awaiting what would happen next.

The fire alarm had stopped ringing, but everyone was ordered to stay clear of the high school. It was freezing outside. Deep inside the building, a lone figure moved purposefully through the glowing hallways.

He stopped to peer out the window at the hundreds of cold figures below.

"Fools," he said softly, and took what he had come for.

*The truth must be taken wherever it is to be found, whether it be in
the past or among strange peoples.*
—al-Kindi

Chapter VI

Missing

Shangri-la Mansion, present time

"HERE, BOY!" JACKIE CALLED OUT to Wolfe, her breath ragged
from a long run in Whispering Woods, the nature preserve that
abutted Shangri-la, her aunt Isobel's mansion by the sea.

Wolfe took his time coming out of the woods; he was busy
sniffing at nearly every tree, taking care to mark his territory
and remind all wildlife that this land was, in fact, his. By most
accounts, he was not a pretty dog. His matted fur was a nondescript
gray, and he had an awkward gait. But he was Jackie's connection
to her former life—when her parents were actually home, and not
tracking Devon—and as such, Wolfe remained her best friend. He
also loved to run with her, and Jackie smiled as she remembered
how he had scrabbled up and down the sand dunes as she ran high
up on the bluffs this afternoon.

Jon had promised to meet her after school for a run, but he had
to pick up his brother, Petey. The seventh grader was staying late to
compete in chess competitions, and their mother, home from the

hospital for only a week now, was still not cleared to drive. Petey was reluctant to stay after school—he didn't want to admit it, but since Mrs. Durrie's brush with death, he liked to come straight home. She had pushed him to resume his after-school activities, and the chess club was, in fact, his favorite—in large part because his current crush was its president. He'd missed the after-school bus today because he'd waited with her for her mom to pick her up.

"Next time you stay late because of Ms. Hot Brainiac, *please* ask for a ride home too, okay?" Jon had sighed, annoyed at his brother. He had just driven up to Jackie's house when Petey had called.

"Well, at least he seems to be bouncing back," Jackie had pointed out. "We'll run together tomorrow." She gave Jon a quick hug, and then bounded back up the marble front steps. "See you in a bit!"

Now, Jackie thought of how Mrs. Durrie had been on the brink of death, and of how she and Jon had brewed a bitter potion that she'd brought back from eighteenth-century Brazil on another of her journeys through time. The concoction revived Jon's mother, much to her oncologist's surprise. In all her years of treating cancer patients, Dr. Mahmood had never seen a patient so far gone experience a full remission, and she said as much to Jon.

"I'm starting to believe in miracles," the oncologist had told him on the day of his mother's discharge, easing Mrs. Durrie into a wheelchair while Petey fiddled with the foot pedals. "Just in time for the holiday season!" They were all feeling festive, and in fact the whole floor had turned out to cheer the single mother of two. Against all odds, she had made it; she was cancer-free.

"Who would believe it, Wolfe?" The old dog's ears pricked up, and he trotted over for attention. She knelt and gave him a hug. "That cure was more than two hundred years old!" Jackie could still see Elva, the medicine women she'd encountered in a community of runaway slaves in eighteenth-century Brazil. It all turned out well, but … She shuddered, trying to suppress images of the slave ship she'd been on. And then a great wave of sadness rolled over her as she thought about her parents, from whom she'd been pulled back to the present. "I wonder where they are now," she mused.

"Jackie! *Venha ca!* Come here! It's *muito frio*—very cold—outside! You'll catch pneumonia, and then what good are you?" Aunt Isobel's Brazilian housekeeper, Dona Marta, had poked her head out the door.

But Jackie was still warm from the run, and she took her time stretching, reveling in the afterglow of exertion. She kicked out her lean, long legs, clad in dark running tights with reflective swirls at her ankles. "Aw, how girlie," Jon had teased her the first time he had seen those tights, a gift from Aunt Isobel.

The eccentric art dealer was very pleased that her niece had come out of her sullen shell and was joining school sports and clubs. Isobel L'eroux had neither the time nor inclination to watch a muddy cross-country race, but she encouraged Jackie's efforts in the best way that she knew: she happily ordered running gear for her thriving niece.

"I'll show you girlie," Jackie had said, taking a menacing step toward the tall young man.

"No, no! Not the pressure points!" Jon had only half feigned fear. Jackie had demonstrated her advanced black-belt techniques on him not long after they met. She'd made the smallest movement, and he'd ended up on the floor, promising to never doubt the authenticity of the martial arts training she'd received before she came to Arborville. Not for the first time, she missed training at the dojo. But her old life was gone now; there was no question about that.

As she stomped through the lightly packed snow to the ornately carved back door that presided over a large wooden deck, she thought about her new life in Aunt Isobel's care. When she first came to Arborville after her parents' accident, she'd had only two choices: withdraw from the world, mired in depression, or get out of bed and take each day as it came. The former wasn't really an option, not with Aunt Isobel's get-up-and-go attitude. The globetrotting art and antiques dealer was not going to let her sister's child simply waste away her life. "The key to feeling better is to be productive. Therefore, I advise keeping busy," Isobel had told her, and Jackie had followed her advice.

Jackie also found solace in her regular runs through Whispering Woods. No matter how bad she felt starting out, she always felt better by the time she returned. Now she braced herself against the oversized door and loosened her laces before she stepped inside Shangri-la.

"You've a visitor, dearest," Aunt Isobel called out from the mansion's enormous library.

Jackie removed her shoes. "You mean, besides you?" she teased. Isobel L'eroux, art dealer to the rich and famous, was hardly ever home. "It's the thrill of the chase, you know," she'd once confided in Jackie. "Getting to the piece before your competitors. But it's also the discovery of the unknown." She'd paused. "It's the unexpected find that really has the most meaning to me." Jackie knew that Isobel kept many of her "unexpecteds"—the house looked like a working museum.

"Yo, doll, what are you, crazy? You chasing Frosty the Snowman or what?" Anthony had sunk deep into an oversized chair. "You keep that up and you'll damage your ovaries!"

Jackie winced; she never knew what would come out of Anthony's mouth. Fortunately, Aunt Isobel had gone into the kitchen to check on dinner. "You keep that up, Anthony, and you'll damage your mouth," she retorted.

"Oh yeah, how's that?" He clasped his hands behind his head and grinned.

"When my fist goes through it, that's how." She sat on the rug and continued her stretching.

"Yeah, yeah, I'm real scared of you," he said lazily. Stretched over her left leg, she looked up at him.

Anthony cleared his throat and sat a bit straighter. "Okay, maybe I am." He knew she had a black belt in jujitsu, and some of the basic techniques she'd demonstrated on him worked very well indeed. He winced at the memory. "Anyway, we gotta get our work done. So I rode out here an hour ago—you didn't tell me you were living in a friggin' palace."

It was practically true. The grounds of Shangri-la encompassed fifty acres, and the house itself was so large that Jackie had her own wing, which included a bedroom, living room, study area, and full bath.

"That must have been some long bike ride," she replied. He lived at the other end of town, at least ten miles away. "How'd you know where to find me? Jon?"

Though Jackie and Anthony had become fast friends in the last month or so and were in the same classes, they had only ever hung out at school or in town. Shangri-la was such a grand mansion that it was virtually in its own neighborhood, which Jackie found a little embarrassing. Of all her school friends, only Jon knew where she lived. Until now.

Anthony nodded. "Yeah. I hope that's okay." He glanced around the richly decorated room. "The project is due at the end of the week. I don't like surprises—things come up, you know." That was certainly true in his case. He never knew when he'd be called on to help out at home with the younger kids or go to work with his dad, when he would have the chance to make a few bucks at the bakery. "There's no homework due tomorrow. We have some time."

"Yeah, sure," Jackie said. Anthony was right, and she was glad that he was here so they could get some work done. "It's too bad Jon didn't give you a ride, though. It's freezing out." She knew he could count on no one else; his other so-called friends would have tortured him for being so studious. But no one ever scoffed at him for being friends with Jon, whom everyone respected for his easy charm and strong work ethic. She could sense that deep down, Anthony aspired to be like the tall runner. She hoped he could gain the confidence to break away from the friends who mocked him.

"You're telling me," Anthony replied. "That loser ignored my texts." He gave Jackie a grin, which she returned. Jon was a good friend to them both.

Jackie touched her toes once more and then reached skyward with both hands, giving her spine a satisfying stretch. "I checked out a great book today. It has everything we need. Here … It's in my backpack." She got up slowly, mindful of her sore legs but happy she'd had a tough workout. "I'll get it."

But Anthony wasn't paying attention; he was reading his text messages. One caught his eye, and he turned on the floor lamp to read it again. "Holy mother of …"

As she riffled through her backpack, Jackie remembered his distraction in school—one of his text messages had bothered him. She wondered if this one was from the same sender. She was about to ask him about it when she had a surprise of her own. She checked her backpack once more.

"Anthony," she said quietly, "the book is gone."

Untruth naturally afflicts historical information.
—Ibn Rushd

Chapter VII

Far Beyond the Silk Roads

Baghdad, 927 CE

No one paid much attention to the foreigner as he made his
way through the outer quarters of the city. Baghdad bustled with
new folk every day, pouring in not only from all of Dar al-Islam
but also from western and eastern Europe—indeed, from as far
away as China—and this had been true for hundreds of years.
Ever since the Han emperor Wu-di, "the Martial Emperor," had
pursued the development of the Silk Roads to the west, Baghdad
had been an important stopping point for those traveling between
Beijing and Byzantium, and, naturally, for those on far less arduous
journeys.

Many of those seeking quarter here sought knowledge; this was
their exotic "good," rather than the silk and spices, the ivory and
glass that were traded openly in any of the town's marketplaces.
Since the founding of Baghdad in the eighth century, and with the

creation of the House of Wisdom not long afterward, libraries and schools had flowered. The love of learning had spread throughout the Islamic empire and was nurtured, in particular, in Baghdad.

"How can you tell a native of Baghdad? He is distinguished by his love of learning," rather than outward appearance, the saying went. Baghdad housed Arab, Persian, Chinese, and African Muslims; Christians and Jews, whom Muslims called the People of the Book, were welcome, as were Zoroastrians, Hindus, and Buddhists, and Europeans from as far away as England came seeking knowledge.

Now the foreigner picked his way through what would be to the casual observer an impossible maze of alleys, and came at last upon his boarding place. He spoke to no one, and by his busy and distracted air, it was clear that he did not welcome conversation. As he made his way toward the back entrance stair, however, a tiny eye-level window in the dark, heavy wooden door at the foot of the stairs slid open.

"Your rent is due, stranger." A dark eye peered out at the man, who kept his head bowed; he wore a turban so large that it nearly blocked his vision. He clutched his robes and stopped.

The landlord's widow was suspicious. The man seemed to be carrying a package beneath the bulk of his robes—but why the furtive movements? The dark eye narrowed. "Well?"

"Another day and you shall have double," the stranger said. He kept his head down.

The eye narrowed further; it was almost a slit. "Why double? I ask only what is fair. I must feed my children, you know."

The stranger lifted his head to face her. He was pale, clearly from the northern lands, and his weasel-like features did not invite further talk. His narrow face seemed more pinched than usual; a greasy strand of light yellow hair escaped his turban. He—Devon—looked his landlady full in the face.

"Mohammed preached charity; is not this one of the pillars of Islam?" His gaze held steady.

The eyehole slid shut, and Devon heard whispering behind the door. He knew that the landlady lived with her mother and her five children; her husband, a former member of al-Mansur's army, had been killed in an ambush just outside the walls of Baghdad. He knew too that she had several solid tenants, so he didn't feel too bad for the woman. And as a woman with no brothers, and therefore no protectors, she did not have much room to maneuver here.

The tiny door slid open. "Tomorrow." She looked down to where Devon was clutching at his robe. "May Allah have mercy on your soul." Then the door slammed shut, and all was silent.

Devon took the stairs two at a time and pushed open the crude door that led to his room.

"Damn!" Once the door slammed shut behind him, he ripped off his turban and flung it on the bed. He never knew how to wind it about his head properly and wasn't even sure if it mattered. There were many different types of people and dress in Baghdad, but he thought a robe and a turban would be the simplest way to disguise the fact that he was really a traveler from the twenty-first century.

Devon knew of the routes merchants, scholars, and pilgrims had taken to find their way to this teeming city, from dhows that sailed the monsoons in the Indian Ocean, the "Land Beneath the Winds," to the arduous journey along the Silk Roads north or south of the Taklamakan Desert; the trek from China was quite perilous indeed.

He laughed to think of how he had moved through time using the age-old knowledge contained in a book. Though Samarkand, where the book had originated, was a stop along the ancient overland journey, he had come from a greater distance, indeed: twenty-first-century America. "Now, that's way beyond the Silk Road!" he snorted.

He carefully removed two books from beneath his robes. One he went to set aside immediately; this was the volume he'd lifted from Professor Tempo's home so many years—lifetimes, really—ago.

"Ow!" The ancient book from Samarkand glowed, hot to the touch; its swirling cover design appeared to come to life. Devon knew from past experience that this meant the book was signaling him, but he wasn't about to pay attention to it now.

"I am *not* leaving now—not after all this time!" He had made so much progress in recent days. It had taken him far too long to get a bearing on his surroundings, and he had finally established a faithful network of those who would serve his great ambition. He smiled again. They would be rewarded beyond their wildest dreams.

Devon set the book down and turned his attention to the second volume, which had all the information he needed to handle his current situation.

"*Infinite Knowledge, Eternal Life,*" he said thoughtfully, and lay down on his pallet to read, heedless of the darkening of the skies, of the mournful calls to prayer that echoed from minarets throughout the city as night fell.

Devon had a keen mind and a photographic memory, and he read steadily and thoroughly through the night, stopping only to refill the small oil lantern; apart from the radiance of the ancient book, this was his main source of light. As the first blush of dawn crept across the early-morning sky, he pressed his lips into a thin line that passed for a smile, and threw open his dark wooden shutters to welcome yet another warm day in Baghdad.

His plan was complete. There was no stopping him now. He cast a scornful look at the book from Samarkand, which had glowed steadily through the night, ironically providing him with yet another possible source of illumination even as he ignored it.

"I might not need you anymore," Devon said as he shoved the book aside, recoiling from its heat. He lay back down on his pallet, this time to rest and prepare for the long day ahead.

Don't grieve. Anything you lose comes back in another form.
—Rumi

Chapter VIII

Arabesque

Shangri-la Mansion, present time

"What do you mean, it's not there?" Anthony stared at Jackie, dumbfounded. "You said you put it right in your backpack." He backed off at her stricken look. "Ah, it's no big deal. The project's not due till Thursday. You probably left it in the library."

From the main section of Shangri-la, the doorbell chimed, a high-pitched tinkling sound that echoed through the house. They both ignored it, lost in thought.

"No—impossible," Jackie said, shaking her head. "It was in my backpack when we were in world history. I meant to keep it home yesterday and do some work from it, but I had a question on one of the readings for Ms. Thompson, so I brought it with me. I swear I saw it in my backpack today, right next to my social studies binder. But I never took it out. Then we had the fire drill, and I forgot all about it."

"So you never took it out at all?" Anthony scratched his head. "Sister, you're totally losing it."

"I totally agree." An annoyed Jon stepped into the library. He ignored Anthony and directed his remarks to Jackie. He took in her running tights and T-shirt, her sweaty hair still pulled back into a high ponytail. "You're not ready?" The tall senior crossed his arms and waited.

Jackie winced and clapped a hand to her head. "Oh my God, I am so sorry, I really am." She whirled to face Anthony, who looked as if he wanted to disappear. "Jon and I were supposed to go downtown tonight. There's some Iranian music festival going on at the library—a really cool group is performing classical Persian music. Do I still have time to—" Jon shook his head, annoyed. "I ran longer than expected—totally lost track of time—and Anthony had to wait around so we could work on our project and—"

"Dinner's ready," Aunt Isobel called out, her voice drifting in before her. Jackie glanced nervously at Jon, but he had relaxed his angry posture as her aunt came in.

It was hard not to smile at the sight of Isobel L'eroux. The petite, if slightly plump, woman was still incredibly beautiful, though she was well into her fifties. Her white hair was coiled high atop her head, and her light purple eyes radiated a keen intelligence. Her clothing was always unique, as well, and often reflected the lands she'd just visited. Today she wore a loose flowing dress that covered her tiny ankles and swept the floor; the rich fabric was decorated by a subtle, repetitive pattern that seemed vaguely familiar to the teens. A large fringed shawl was draped around her shoulders.

She looked at the teens with a faint air of amusement. "Well?" She smiled slightly. The tension in the room was thick, and she suspected teenage angst. "What's the matter?" She glanced meaningfully from Jackie to Jon. Narrowing her eyes, she settled her gaze on Anthony and raised a questioning eyebrow. "Anthony?"

"It's not what you think, Ms. L'eroux." Anthony had jumped to his feet when she entered the room. She was an approachable person who had gone out of her way to welcome him to Shangri-la a few hours earlier, but he was still more than a little intimidated by the owner of this grand house.

"Anthony?" Jackie gasped. "Of course not!"

Jon grinned; he knew better. "It's all good, Ms. L'eroux. Seriously. It's just that Jackie and I are going to miss an event at the library." He rolled his eyes and cracked a smile. "Of course, she got 'lost' running in the Woods."

"The Persian musicians?" Isobel asked. "There's time—I'm going myself; we can all ride together, if you like." She glanced at Jackie. "You really must get cleaned up, dearest. Hurry!"

"But—" Jackie started to protest, but Isobel cut her off.

"I insist." She turned to the boys. "You will eat with me now, and Jackie will take her food in the car."

Anthony found his voice. "Excuse me, Ms. L'eroux." He pointed to Jackie's backpack. "Jackie's missing a book, a really important book that we need for our world history project that's due later this week. She thinks she brought it home—"

"I know I brought it home!" Jackie interrupted.

"—but it's missing now." Anthony walked over to one of the built-in floor-to-ceiling bookshelves. "Any chance it could be here?" He squatted down and began rummaging through the books.

"Anthony, let's just go," Jackie told him.

He ignored her and stared at all the books, whistling as he stood back. "This is a great collection—truly amazing."

Isobel smiled. "Why, thank you, my dear young man."

"Hey!" Anthony peered at one of the worn spines on a lower shelf. "Here it is!" He pulled out the book and opened it up to page one. "Wow, what language is this? It looks familiar—"

"No!" Jackie, Isobel, and Jon reached to retrieve the book from his grasp. Anthony looked up, puzzled. "But this is really cool stuff—really cool!" He peered at the text, lifting it to his face for a closer look. "The words—and pictures—they look like they're moving!"

Suddenly he swayed and stumbled forward, dizzy. "Ow!" He dropped the book on the thick Persian carpet. "Hot!"

Jackie dove in to get it and snatched it up before Jon could move. She tripped in the process, knocking Anthony over.

Instantly she and Anthony disappeared.

The swirling, ceaseless pattern of the Persian carpet seemed to wind itself around Jackie's ankles, and then it was as if she were falling through a great void, a darkness so complete that she wasn't visible at all, not even to herself. But all her other senses were intact: she could feel; she could hear; she could smell; and, it seemed, she could taste (*the bitter brew of time,* she thought).

She stretched her arms and fingers wide, her knees drawn up in a defensive posture, protecting her chest. Her fingers brushed up against something—someone—and she heard Anthony yell out beside her: "No-o-o-o-o—"

He was cut off abruptly, and she heard a loud thud, as if a heavy sack of flour had been thrown onto a cold stone floor.

Then Jackie heard Jon and Aunt Isobel: "Not again! Not now!" "We must stay calm. This was meant to be." "I need to go after them!" "No. We will know when we're needed." "But—" "Have faith. Trust. Believe." "I don't know what to believe—" This last was from Jon, anguish clearly evident in his voice. "I really can't take it anymore."

Jackie reached out again as if to touch him, straining harder to make contact. Suddenly, everything sped up and she felt herself hurtling through inky darkness so fast, so hard, she could barely breathe. She heard wails, mournful and melodic; she whipped through a hundred thousand conversations in a hundred thousand languages. She thought she heard a child whimpering in the darkness, but the sound was so fleeting, she wasn't sure.

And then she knew nothing.

Living life tomorrow's fate, though thou be wise,
Thou canst not tell nor yet surmise;
Pass, therefore, not today in vain,
For it will never come again.
—Omar Khayyam

Chapter IX

Hidden in Plain Sight

Baghdad, 927 CE

"I TELL YOU, ACHMED, IT was the strain of his translation efforts that did him in." The speaker's eyes were barely visible above the cloth that wound around his head and neck. A sudden sandstorm swept through the streets of Baghdad, kicking up a wild dust that threatened passersby, whirling like a dervish as it assaulted the unfortunates still out on the streets. Umar kept his gaze low as he addressed his old teacher, who was dressed in a similar manner; he, too, bowed against the wind. "Do you not agree?"

Achmed motioned his companion to a nearby door, shuttered against the howls of the dry, hot wind. He banged once, and the door swung open immediately. The two scholars stepped down, stooping through the small door, into a short passageway that led to a warm, snug room. An oil lamp lit up a far corner, and Umar could see through the arched doorway beside it; this home was more spacious than it initially appeared.

"Thank you, Mama," Achmed said, gently addressing the wizened old woman who let them in.

Though only her eyes were visible through the narrow opening in her *hijab,* or head covering, Umar could see that she was very old from the way they crinkled, splintering into a thousand folds beside each eye. He could not see her mouth, but he guessed she was smiling; judging from her gentle words, he was right.

"Ah, my brave scholar, you have taken refuge in your old home rather than in your beloved books," she said to Achmed, with not a little amusement tingeing her tone. "Come, I will bring you some tea."

She neither addressed nor looked at Umar; nor did Achmed bother to introduce the other scholar to her. This was his mother, after all, and though she was long widowed and many years past the beauty he remembered from his childhood, he could not have an outsider let his gaze fall upon her. That would be sinful, as any true believer would know. He waited until his mother had left the room, long skirts trailing on the floor behind her. He gave a small grunt of satisfaction as she left. Every part of her body save her eyes was covered. He was proud to have such a virtuous mother.

Achmed motioned to the pillows carefully arranged on the thick Persian rug. "Please," he said, indicating that his colleague should make himself comfortable. The two men sat down with care, mindful of the dust they'd brought in.

Umar settled in and waited. Achmed was famous for his mysterious ways, but he was a brilliant man, one of the finest minds that had ever graced the House of Wisdom.

"Mohammed was working on an important translation," said Achmed, "and it is true that the effort tired him immensely. He was, in fact, quite old—nearly eighty years of age, praise Allah for his long, ripe life." Achmed toyed with one of the folds of his robes. Then he grew still.

"But . . . ?" Umar pressed.

"But he was a strong man, healthy as an ox. His heart was good. His vision was good, although his hearing was not quite what it used to be. At any rate, Mohammed's tribe was known for astounding longevity, and we ourselves knew of the precision of his mind, even at his advanced age." Achmed's sharp eyes pierced his friend. "The strain of his efforts did not kill him."

Umar felt uncomfortable, and he longed for the cool interior of the main study room in the House of Wisdom. He felt the walls of this cozy home crowd in on him.

"So—," he started to blurt, impatient and not like a true scholar at all.

Just then Achmed's mother came in with two cups of hot chai, and he held his tongue and his gaze, staring instead into the depths of the aromatic tea in his hands. She left again.

"So what could have happened?" Umar's mind was racing.

"Oh, it's simple." Achmed leaned back among the cushions, one leg flung out, the other bent casually at the knee.

Umar waited.

"Mohammed was poisoned."

Why do you stay in prison when the door is wide open?
—Rumi

Chapter X

Passages

Baghdad, 927 CE

THE ALCHEMIST PEERED SUSPICIOUSLY AT the instructions before him. "This is not standard procedure," he said.

"Oh please!" His impatient customer paced the small confines of the laboratory. "Did we not strike an agreement? Did you not receive an advance of more dinars today than you've ever seen in your life? You're a scientist—just follow the directions!" His voice rose, unpleasantly shrill. "We had a deal! Must I go elsewhere, or would you like to become a truly wealthy man?" A few blond locks had straggled from his turban, plastered to his forehead with sweat. "Or do I need to reveal the true nature of your *regular*"—here the stranger paused to sneer—"work to the authorities?"

The alchemist paled; his dark skin took on a grayish tinge. "No," he said quietly. "You do not." He paused. "But the instructions are not in accordance with proper laboratory procedures, and that is why I question them."

"What!" Devon exclaimed. His head was spinning. What did the alchemist mean—how could the man know about lab procedure? Had he miscalculated the era? Devon's mind raced; he knew that tremendous strides in science and medicine had occurred during the Abbasid dynasty, but could not pin down the exact date. Under his robe, bound to his waist, the book he'd nicked long ago from Professor Tempo began to warm up. He groaned inwardly. This was a signal; either this ancient tome from Samarkand was about to whisk him off to yet another place and time, or it was sending him an urgent message. *Not now,* he thought silently.

The alchemist waited patiently. When it seemed that his strange customer had sorted out his thoughts, he began to explain.

"Good sir," he started calmly, as if soothing a baby, "you know that above all else—save Allah and family—we Muslims prize learning, and this has been especially true since the reign of Caliph Harun al-Rashid. Now his son, al-Ma'mun, has constructed one of the finest library palaces, which we call Bayt al-Hikma, the House of Wisdom. It is here that some of the greatest advances in math and science have been made, and in recent years, proper laboratory procedure has been developed for men of science."

The alchemist turned to retrieve what looked like a small manual. "Here. This is an example of a procedure that I follow quite commonly, and the instructions are laid out thusly: Directions, Materials, Procedure. The reason is to establish a standard and to ensure accuracy. The directions must not be deviated from, lest there be dire results."

Devon thought back to his high school days and how much he had hated doing labs—mostly because he had to follow directions. He had much preferred mixing ingredients together and watching what happened, like the time he had singed off his lab partner's eyebrows. She'd been pretty upset, and the would-be heir to the Pearson family fortune was booted from yet another private boarding school, but it was worth the look on the snobby girl's face. He chuckled at the memory.

"Sir?" The alchemist awaited Devon's instructions.

"Fine," Devon snapped, miserably aware of the oppressive heat. "Can you come up with a 'standard procedure' soon?"

The alchemist looked doubtful. "I'm not sure. What you've asked of me is highly unusual." He looked at Devon. "But intriguing," he added hopefully. "Come back in two days' time. I'm not quite sure of the result, but it seems that it would be quite interesting."

Devon nodded and left the tiny lab at the back of a spice store. With the back of his hand, he wiped away a thin film of sweat that had collected above his upper lip. "You have no idea," he snarled softly. The customers in the shop moved aside quickly as he made his way out of the store, but he was talking to no one in particular.

"You have no idea."

* * *

Shahan awoke with a start, his head protesting against a pain that had not dulled since he had been brought here several days ago. The dank humidity of the dungeon threatened to choke him with its oppressive weight.

The young scholar put his hand to his brow; his ragged turban was coming undone. He carefully wound the cloth around his head, steeling himself against the pitiful cries of a prisoner being tortured in a nearby cell. He would be next, he was sure of it, for stumbling upon an ancient secret so powerful that it would change the course of humankind—forever. He frowned and rubbed his throbbing temple, aware that one part of the secret was no longer safeguarded in his turban. Whoever knocked him out had surely made off with the secret writings; he had been followed, he was certain, ever since he'd told Achmed about the mysterious document he'd recently translated.

"I went through it at least five times," Shahan had insisted, "and cross-checked the piece with the work of Galen, who had referenced but not verified the procedure. Shocking, wouldn't you agree?"

Achmed had stroked his long, curling beard, eyes narrowing. "I find it hard to believe that the ancient Greeks would give such an idea credence. Above all else, the Greek philosophers were lovers of Truth, as their profession indicated, and the theory you've just described seems too fanciful to be true, even for a poet such as myself."

Shahan nodded. He was a slight man, not even twenty years of age, young to have so much access to the documents occupying the House of Wisdom, Baghdad's finest library and center of scholarship. But Shahan's keen intellect and translation skills were legendary; by the time he was seven, he'd mastered five classical languages. At age twelve, he'd helped to translate the works of Euclid, and at sixteen was invited to present the ideas of Pythagoras to a small audience that included the caliph al-Ma'mun. The caliph was so impressed that he insisted Shahan be given full standing to assist in the translation of myriad documents that had been brought from Byzantium a few years before.

"We need the finest minds to decipher the works of the world's first philosophers, so that we might build on their ideas." Al-Ma'mun did not want to lose the young Shahan to a competing House of Wisdom; he'd heard that the scholar from Central Asia had received an invitation to reside at the library in Alexandria and conduct his studies from there. So he offered the brilliant young man a permanent position as assistant to the library director, a decision that rankled some of the senior scholars. The library director was the most powerful man in the House of Wisdom, save the caliph himself, and all those who worked under him were granted first and ready access to all the documents to be studied and translated.

Shahan sighed. He was a long way away from Alexandria—and truth be told, from the Baghdad he knew, though he was currently residing in the bowels of the ancient city.

He looked around. Most of the prisoners, like him, were shackled to the walls—like in Plato's *Allegory of the Cave,* he thought. A few lay inert on the firmly packed dirt ground, and it seemed to Shahan that they were dead.

"You!" The deep voice of a tall African guard, bare from the waist up, startled him out of his musings. The man's white teeth glistened in the half darkness of the prison. Shahan's heart beat violently against his chest; it seemed to him that he would die of fear before they racked the secret out of him. Not for the first time in his life, Shahan wished he were skilled in the art of fighting. *Not that it would matter here,* he thought miserably. Even if he did break free, there was no place for him to run.

The burly man bent over with a grunt to unshackle Shahan's leg chain. The prisoner instinctively reached down to rub it; he'd recently uncovered some Greek documents on the circulation of blood, and it made sense as a way to restore health to his leg.

"On your feet—now!" The prison guard jerked Shahan to standing with one swift move. The scholar's legs nearly buckled beneath him with fright. The man was a giant. The end was near, he was sure of it, and he needed to prepare himself for a glorious death. He began to pray fervently. "Oh merciful Allah, I have sought only to do your bidding and to use my skills to promote your greater glory for all of Dar al-Islam, and I—"

Frightened, he started to retch. The prison guard pushed him along, past the other moaning prisoners, who looked at him beseechingly, some so far gone that their eyes had rolled back in their heads.

"Glory be to Allah," whispered Shahan, stumbling along. They had come to a large, heavy wooden door that was studded with metal bolts. The hinges were clearly the work of a superior blacksmith, Shahan couldn't help but notice, and then he realized the absurdity of his thought. He was about to die. The door swung open slowly, and the guard pushed him through.

"He's not too damaged, eh?" a mildly amused voice said, piercing Shahan's deep misery. His knees sagged, and firm hands lifted him up and across the threshold. "Ah, the resilience of the young. You'll be fine. Come, let us make you presentable, as befitting one of Baghdad's finest resident scholars."

Shahan looked up at the speaker, confused. Dark eyes twinkled kindly at the young man.

"You've an audience with the caliph himself."

The World is three days: As for yesterday, it has vanished, along with all that was in it. As for tomorrow, you may never see it. As for today, it is yours, so work in it.
—Hassan al-Basri

Chapter XI

Faithless Intruders

SHE WAS FLOATING ON A sea of clouds, endless, soft, and deep, that shifted and gently gave way beneath her as she moved, stretching, luxuriating in their comfort. She drifted, surfacing to consciousness and then submerging into slumber and back up again. Yet something tugged at the edges of her awareness; she needed to wake up.

Jackie felt a slight pressure on her eyelids—quick, simple strokes, and a tug at the edges. Someone was applying makeup to her. She forced her lashes apart and stared uncomprehendingly at the scene before her.

"Look, she awakens," came a quick cry, and then a hush swept through the half-dozen women who peered down at her.

"Her eyes are green—imagine!"

"That's not so terribly unusual."

"Yes, the caliph had a slave girl in his harem from Caucasus, and her eyes were green as well."

"Her hair was yellow, was it not?"

"Indeed. But she was not a pretty thing. I don't know what Pasha could have seen in her. Her face was always red—from crying, no doubt."

"You'd cry, too, if you were a slave girl in a foreign land!" The women laughed and nudged each other knowingly.

A cool, quiet voice broke in: "Unless you were as strong and wise as Umm al-Muqtadir. Though she was no slave girl when she was brought here in the flower of her beauty, she hailed from faraway Byzantium. We are—each of us, in our own way—all from foreign lands, but unified under Dar al-Islam."

"Yes, *qahramana*," the other women assented.

Jackie watched carefully, knowing full well that she needed to assess her surroundings before she made a move. Clearly the one they called the *qahramana* was in a position of authority, a stewardess of sorts, and they continued to defer to her now as she began to issue orders on how best to dispense of Jackie.

"Go now, straight to Umm al-Muqtadir, and make haste," said the qahramana, a raven-haired beauty. "And in the name of Allah, avoid the chamberlain! We don't need him running to the vizier about our … situation. I do so hate unpleasantness in our harem."

Jackie froze. Our *harem*? She fought down panic and very real fear at the thought of where she was and what might be in store for her. Was that why they were applying makeup to her? Was she supposed to be some man's … love slave, should he choose her? She had to get out of here!

Jackie clenched her teeth and forced herself to confront her surroundings, expecting to see pinched and miserable faces of women who had long suffered this fate, imprisoned by the man who had chosen them. But instead she saw a lively group, all very beautiful, it was true, who seemed very curious about the stranger in their midst. She noticed that the room opened up into a larger space, some sort of courtyard, and she could hear the splashing of water—a fountain perhaps?—and the laughter of children. The harem didn't seem very much like a prison at all, but a very busy place where select women and their children went about their daily activities. In fact, the qahramana herself carried a beautiful boy of about three on her hip. He regarded her silently as he sucked his thumb.

Now what? Jackie groaned to herself as the women discussed her looks. It was clear that they didn't expect her to join in their conversation, which was fine with Jackie. She needed time to think. She tried to sit up straighter, and immediately twelve hands reached to support her. It was only then that she realized she'd been nestled on luxurious silk and brocade cushions—and not floating on clouds, as she'd dreamed.

Now the women around her leaned in, affording Jackie an even closer look at them as well. Their dark hair hung thick and loose, well past their waists. There was no question that they were quite beautiful. They wore long, flowing pants, topped by long-sleeved, silken tunics that hung down to their knees.

"Here, let me touch up her kohl," said an almond-eyed beauty, who turned to dip a thin brush into a small pot of black paste.

"Oh, please, Fatima," said the qahramana, "she is not your plaything." Jackie looked up at the stewardess of the harem, intrigued by her gold-flecked eyes. "The last time you lined *my* lids, I looked like a common tramp." The others nodded.

"But she's so unusual. Look at her hair!" Fatima murmured, her brush hovering above Jackie's right eye. "She's like an exotic little doll; anyway, I just can't resist."

Jackie's hand shot out and closed around the makeup artist's slender wrist as the young woman swooped in to further decorate her eyelids. "No."

"*Ai!*" Fatima was locked in her grip, and the other women froze.

Jackie stood up carefully, still holding fast to the young woman's delicate wrist, and was mindful not to stumble on the cushions. Her bare feet sank deep into the thick Persian carpet. She glanced down and started in surprise.

Her feet were covered in swirling, hennaed designs; it was then that she looked carefully at her hands and arms as the sleeves of her own tunic fell back. These were covered in intricate designs as well.

"What ... is this place? And ... what have you done to me?" She released Fatima, who set down the beauty tools she was about to wield on Jackie.

The girls looked at each other in surprise. This newest girl was bold. For a recent addition to the caliph's harem, she was also rather unafraid.

"And where ... where is my book?" Jackie searched her surroundings in a hurry, keeping a wary eye on the women, lest they approach with more beauty tips.

"Do you mean this?" One of the younger women had spirited it away while Jackie was recovering consciousness. She pulled the book from a safe place under her bed and handed it over.

"Yes! Thank you!" Jackie hugged the book to her chest.

"Strange," said a new voice. A regal woman had entered the room during the commotion; now all the women fell back in deep respect. In spite of her advanced age, Umm al-Muqtadir was clearly the most arresting woman of the group. She had high, striking cheekbones, and her black eyes glinted as she stared thoughtfully at Jackie. Her heavy raven hair was shot through with gray. She tilted her head, gazing thoughtfully at the book and then back at Jackie. "I have been told that we couldn't open it at all." She smoothed the front of her yellow silken tunic and looked down, plucking at an imaginary thread.

Jackie nodded and held the book tighter. It was her guide and would help explain what she was doing here in a small room full of women and rich tapestries. It was also, she knew from past experience, her way out. The book would respond to no one else.

"Perhaps Caliph al-Muqtadir would like to look at it," piped a young girl, who had been sitting cross-legged on a large pillow with swirling designs. Jackie nearly jumped out of her skin. She hadn't seen the little girl before. The child continued, "Because he really likes books and likes to collect all kinds, too!"

"You would presume to know the caliph's mind?" Umm al-Muqtadir gave the child a severe look, and the women lowered their eyes.

"Of course, only you, the royal mother, know what is best for the caliph." Fatima drew the child, her daughter, to her plump body. "I mean ... naturally ... he has his own mind, but is ever wise to take counsel from the one who bore him many moons ago—"

"Thank you," the qahramana interrupted with her smooth voice, "thank you, mother of our most cherished caliph, for your clarity and guidance in this and all other matters. We all know what befalls those who do not appreciate your wisdom."

The caliph's mother stifled a yawn. "Yes—pity about the last vizier, no? He tried to bribe his way out of his cell, but his jailer"—she nodded at the qahramana—"saw that his punishment for meddling was carried out in full." Fatima blanched and pressed her daughter closer.

By now, Jackie understood that she was in a medieval Muslim world. She was also beginning to sense that the woman who bore the caliph was perhaps the real power behind the throne. She averted her eyes as the imperious Umm al-Muqtadir brought her gaze to bear fully upon her.

"So the book ... and this feisty beauty ... hmm." She tipped Jackie's chin up. "And these eyes—"

Just as Jackie tensed, longing to use some of her basic martial arts training to get the woman out of her face, an upset in the next room startled them all. There was a terrible crash, and then loud screaming ensued. Another shattering, this time possibly of glass. All the women ran out to see.

"Hey! Cut it out!" A young man tried to fend off several angry-looking guards as the caliph's women all dropped back, horrified, and quickly rushed to cover their hair with dark veils.

"A strange man! Oh, we are lost! Quick, my hijab!" They were frantic with fear, Jackie noted with surprise. Someone threw a dark shawl over her head, and she pushed it aside impatiently to get a better view.

The man was seized from behind by two of the guards, who shoved him to the floor. Another put his foot on the intruder's back. She knew that voice, and there was something else familiar about the unwanted visitor, but Jackie couldn't quite tell what it was. Could it be—?

Just then, the man stopped struggling and looked up at her.

"No way!" he said, shocked. A guard cuffed him on the back of the head, and the young man was out like a light. Jackie covered her mouth in shock and stumbled back a step. Fatima caught her and looked up at the redhead, confused.

"I know that man," Jackie whispered.

Indeed she did. It was Anthony.

I didn't come here of my own accord, and I can't leave that way.
Whoever brought me here will have to take me home.
—Rumi

Chapter XII

The Quality of Mercy

"Now look what you've done," Anthony muttered. Even in the plush comfort of the women's quarters, he was thoroughly miserable. He rubbed the back of his head where the guard had hit him, knocking him out. "Ow!"

Jackie bit back a retort. It was technically true that she had set them on an improbable journey to what seemed to be an Islamic city. However, he wasn't making the situation any better with all his dramatics.

After Anthony had been subdued, the chamberlain had interrogated the women harshly as the eunuch guards stood by, demanding to know where Jackie had come from. He had bowed politely as Umm al-Muqtadir swept out of the room, but all the other women were to stay. All but the qahramana had cowered before the chamberlain, who was, in fact, responsible for the goings-on in the women's quarters.

"We assumed she was a new ... ah ... acquisition for the caliph," the elegant woman had replied, standing her ground. "She is quite beautiful, you know." With an imperious wave of her hand, the palace guards, who had been brought in as reinforcements for this breach of security, turned their backs on the women. At her signal, Fatima, who had been standing near, drew away Jackie's hijab.

The chamberlain gasped. "Indeed she is." The short, plump man drew closer, marveling at Jackie's creamy complexion and green eyes. "She is rather thin, so I'm not certain she'll be to his liking, but she is worthy of his viewing, that is certain." He passed a small hand over his bald head, musing over how to go about telling the caliph that a beautiful stranger had suddenly appeared in the women's quarters. Then he thought about her belligerent companion, who lay quite still on the floor. He could have the man executed, but the caliph was bound to find out. And then it would be his own head, as well, for a clear breach of security in the women's quarters—his domain. Certainly there was no love lost between him and Umm al-Muqtadir. Ever since her son had risen to the position of caliph, the chamberlain's life had been a living hell. The woman was quite smart, and her son visited her in her chambers every day to seek her counsel. He needed to get her on his side.

The chamberlain sighed. "Let me think of the best way to handle the red-haired girl. It really depends on his mood."

Jackie felt a surge of white-hot anger. Quite forgetting that she was in a completely foreign place—and time—she shook herself free of Fatima's grasp and glared at the man.

"I am *not* a piece of property, to be bartered and shown off in this way!" She shook with anger, long red curls tumbling over her face. "I *am* foreign, yes, and from a different place, but I am not an object to be treated thusly!" She stopped, wondering why her speech had become so archaic. Jon would have laughed to hear her. *Well, I certainly can't say, "What up, dude?"* she thought ruefully.

The women drew a collective gasp behind her, and Fatima stepped back, physically distancing herself from a potential criminal.

"No, I can see that," said the chamberlain thoughtfully, rubbing his chin. "I think the caliph himself would be quite interested in the book you are gripping so very tightly." He glanced down at Anthony, who was starting to come to. "He does like new distractions—and I think you'd both serve him well."

Jackie shuddered. "No need for fear, child," the man said soothingly. "He is very intellectual, and I think he would like to know from whence you came—and how."

Thus it was that Jackie and Anthony found themselves locked up in a room of unimaginable luxury, with nothing to occupy themselves but each other and the contents of the room itself as they awaited the arrival of the all-important caliph, ruler of the Abbasid dynasty. As he and the qahramana escorted them to their cloistered quarters, the chamberlain had confided that as long as they held Caliph al-Muqtadir's interest, they should come to no harm; the man liked to be entertained.

Jackie's knees had buckled with the news. She had no idea what to expect. She did know from her studies that the Abbasid dynasty was the "Golden Age of Islam": the caliphs al-Rashid and, later, his son al-Ma'mun were most generous patrons of all sorts of scholars, and a premium was put on many types of study. Al-Ma'mun, in particular, was brilliant beyond imagination, fascinated by all manner of learning. On the other hand, she also knew that Muslims were fearless warriors and unmerciful toward unbelievers. Anthony was a devout Catholic, that much she knew. She hoped for his sake that he wouldn't rail against Islam and start saying Hail Marys.

The qahramana lingered upon the chamberlain's departure.

"As chief stewardess to the caliph's mother, I am your official jailer, though there are guards beyond this door. I would have you know that she bears you no ill will in this breach of security, for it seems as if you were as much surprised as we were to find yourselves in the caliphal harem." Without the child on her hip, the qahramana had assumed the full mantle of her authority, and she seemed taller and slightly forbidding. Jackie noticed that she held a set of keys in her hand.

"There seems to be quite a lot in the way of jailers and guards," Jackie observed wryly. "And there's the chamberlain, and a vizier, whom we're about to meet—"

"Yeah, gives a whole new meaning to the word *Byzantine*," Anthony muttered, arms crossed, glancing out the barred keyhole window at the enclosed courtyard one story down. He could see a small boy playing beneath a lemon tree, squatting and holding out a piece of fallen fruit to his mother.

The qahramana frowned and looked at him sharply.

"He means that it seems very complicated here—lots of politics in the way the harem is run," Jackie hastened to explain. "It's certainly not at all what I'd expect … I mean, I thought a harem was a sort of holding pen for all the caliph's women."

Their jailer's frown deepened further. "It's not so complicated," she said, "and certainly not as barbaric as you imply." She crossed her arms, and the sunlight glinted off her silver keys. "The caliph has four wives, because he can care for them, of course, and many concubines. They and their children live here in protection. As you can see, they are well attended indeed, as are those of us who are charged with running the caliphal harem: myself and other qahramanas. We help run the harem and oversee everything from household supplies to the health of its inhabitants. There are several thousand people living here."

"What about the caliph's mother?" Jackie asked.

"Ah, Umm al-Muqdatir. She has the ultimate authority since her son is caliph, and he confers with her nearly every day in her chambers, on all matters—great and small." The qahramana gave a slight smile.

"How do you know that?" Anthony turned from the window, still unhappy with his forced seclusion, but interested now.

"Because it is my responsibility to serve her," replied the beautiful woman.

"Not the caliph?" Jackie was curious.

The qahramana threw her head back and laughed. "Oh no. I have a suitor of my own, and when the time is right, he will ask Umm al-Muqtadir for my hand." She saw Jackie's confused look and anticipated her question. "I have borne no children; the boy I carried about earlier was my sister's." She smiled, her perfect pearly teeth gleaming in the gathering dusk. Not for the first time, Jackie found herself admiring the woman's beauty.

"But how will he get through all of that?" Anthony gestured out the grated window.

The qahramana's eyes twinkled. "Perhaps I'll smuggle him in, like the chief qahramana before me did." Anthony and Jackie looked stunned. "Yes, the story goes that she hid her man in a laundry basket and thus made her way past the guards and eunuchs, until he was able to emerge and plead his case before the caliph's mother. They were married not long after."

"Well, then, can you smuggle us out?" Anthony asked hopefully.

"No," replied the lovely stewardess, "absolutely not." Then she turned on her heel and locked them in.

"Anthony," said Jackie when they were finally alone, "I am so, so sorry. Just—when the vizier gets here, let me do the talking, okay?"

"Ah, sweetheart, don't worry." Anthony gave her a lopsided grin. "Anthony's got you covered."

Jackie rolled her eyes.

"Seriously. Number one, I'm the guy here, *capisce*? And number two, you're Jon's babe, and I owe him everything." Jackie was surprised to see him blink back tears. "Everything." Then he looked up, determined. "Anyway, this is just a dream, so I'm not gonna worry too much about it because—see?—I'm just gonna wake up and it'll all be okay. And then I'll be like, 'Holy crap, I missed the bus again' and then—"

"Hey, could you stop with the tough-guy act? It's just me, not those idiots you show off for at school." Jackie put a finger to his lips. "Let's just look around, okay?"

Anthony hung his head. "You're right; they'll never leave me alone anyway." He gave a tight smile. "I wish I could be more like Jon and not care, but they were my friends when we were kids and—"

"—and now they're failing out of school and are mad that you're not still one of them," Jackie finished. "Is that what those text messages were all about?"

Anthony blew out his cheeks and released the air with a big sigh. "Yeah. Vinny and Tony have been trying to jump me every day. They asked me to hang out last weekend, and when I got near the railroad tracks, where we usually meet, one of them had a baseball bat, and I got the heck out of there." He stared out the window again. "So not only am I a total nerd, but I'm a coward, too."

Jackie clenched her fists, furious for her friend. Anthony noticed and gave a rueful grin.

"Ha. I know you'd beat them up for me, ninja woman," he said. "It's my fight anyway. I just have to deal with it." He looked around the room. "We've got bigger problems to deal with first."

"Agreed," Jackie said with a nod. She glanced at the volumes of books piled high on the low table in the center of the room, and took in the richness of the décor. She idly thumbed through a book.

"Though I gotta tell you"—Anthony looked at her appraisingly—"Jon would love to be here now. You sure do look hot."

Jackie threw him a look, and he shut up. She settled on one of the cushions scattered around the table. She felt a sudden warmth from within the folds of her clothing, pulled out Aunt Isobel's book, and started leafing through the pages.

Anthony backed away. "Oh, nooo, you don't!"

Suddenly, the ornately carved door was pushed open with surprising force, narrowly missing the wall. *Would've made a nice dent,* flashed through Jackie's mind just as a half-dozen burly guards barged into the room.

A thin, finely dressed man in his sixties strode in to meet the prisoners. Jackie shrank back a bit, for his cold, dark eyes seemed to pierce right through her as his gaze swept the room. Somehow, she didn't think he was the caliph; he seemed too businesslike. His eyes fell upon Aunt Isobel's book, which seemed to Jackie to have shrunk in on itself.

"Ah!" said the vizier, chief adviser to the caliph. "There it is." He pointed to the book. "You"—he looked at one of the guards—"bring the book here. We will inspect it and report to Umm al-Muqtadir. She will decide if the caliph should see it or not." He gritted his teeth at the thought that his ruler should be thus held in thrall by a woman, even if she was his mother. *Ah, this is because he has no real work to do,* thought the vizier. Harun Ma'mun had built the great House of Wisdom, and Baghdad was a great center of learning, and the Translation Movement was in full swing. What else could the present caliph do, indeed, but while away his days with his mother and his family? The vizier sighed.

At a nod from the vizier, the confident young guard switched his scimitar to his left hand as he stepped farther into the room and reached down for the book. A ray of sunlight filtered through the long, narrow arched window and glinted off the sword. He never took his eyes off Jackie and Anthony, who had shifted closer together in fear. With his scimitar raised high, threatening to slice off their heads with a single swipe of the blade, the guard reached for the book, which was open at the center; the pages were blank now.

Jackie held her breath. *If he takes the book, there's no way out for us.* She glanced at the open door; Aunt Isobel had told her, long ago it seemed, that the way out was to take the Middle Road to a doorway back home. But Jackie knew full well that beyond this passage more guards awaited. She couldn't see any way out.

The guard's fingers hovered over the book. Jackie closed her eyes.

Thump!

The book snapped shut and shifted a fraction away from the guard. The strong young man hesitated. Jackie noticed the cords in his neck straining with fear. The guard swallowed hard.

"What is this?" the vizier hissed. "Bring the book to me! Now!"

The guard braced himself and grabbed the book. In the next instant, he was on the floor howling and clutching his hand. Smoke curled from his fingers. "I'm on fire! Help me in the name of Allah!" he howled.

After a moment of shock, the vizier snapped his fingers at the stunned guards. "Well? Help him!"

One of the more quick-thinking fellows grabbed a nearby pitcher of water and doused the burning flesh. The injured guard let out a thin wail, and the rest of the guards bustled off with him.

"I see," said the vizier, narrowing his eyes, staring hard now at Jackie. "Well, you are solely responsible for the book. That much is clear."

Jackie nodded, mute. The acrid smell of burning flesh lingered in the air.

"Pick it up."

She did as she was told; the book was still warm, but not uncomfortably so.

"Now you will follow me." The vizier was grim.

Jackie looked at Anthony, who was, for once, stunned into silence. "Let's go," she said. "We really have no choice." She tugged at his sleeve. Anthony nodded; she was right.

With his fierce brows drawn together, the vizier cast a harsh look back at the two teens. "You will explain all this, and to one who will determine your fate." He spun around, robes flying, muttering angrily. "Umm al-Muqtadir was right; we're going to have to use Shahan after all." Then, almost to himself: "How is it that women always know so much?"

And with that, the three of them made their way through a maze of secret passageways, through a courtyard overflowing with the scent of flowers in full bloom, and into yet another building with more passageways. The vizier stopped at the open door of a simple room, sparsely furnished but for an elaborate rug on the floor and a few scattered cushions. On one of those cushions sat a young man. He was so thin that his turban threatened to slide off his head, and his eyes were ringed with fatigue—*or was it fear?* Jackie wondered.

The young man stood to greet them, carefully unfolding his lean frame to do so. He bowed low and deep to the vizier, and then he turned his attention to the book Jackie still grasped in her hand. He bit his lip.

"Yes, sire," he said softly to the vizier, eyes never leaving the book's elaborately decorated cover, "that is the one."

"One what?" Annoyed, Anthony had finally found his voice.

"That book … it is the one"—Shahan hesitated, hardly believing what the girl clutched in her hands—"that was stolen from my father's library." He paused to wipe his brow. "My late father was the most eminent scholar in all of Samarkand."

What you seek is seeking you.
—Rumi

Chapter XIII

Hidden in Plain Sight

THE VIZIER SMIRKED. "INDEED HE WAS. As you are today, Shahan ibn Mamoor." It was hard to tell from his tone whether the powerful official, second only to the caliph himself, was being sarcastic. Still, the young scholar inclined his head, reddening slightly at the remarks.

The vizier turned to a very confused Anthony and Jackie, and the latter clutched her aunt Isobel's book more firmly, pressing it to her chest. In spite of herself, her eyes filled with tears, and she reached up to brush them away, smudging her kohl eyeliner as she did so. Anthony glanced at her sideways, noting her extreme distress, as a line of black kohl ran down one cheek.

"Don't worry—Anthony's got it all under control." He referred to himself in third person, hoping to lighten the mood. "I know what to do—I saw it in the movies."

Jackie knew that all his tough talk was a cover for his fear. With that, he turned to Shahan and the vizier, who were now whispering to each other.

"You, I gotta say, I like your funky robes—you know, I heard of guys wearing dresses, but this is different, and it's cool, you know?" Anthony winked and gave a thumbs-up to the two men, who were staring at him, openmouthed. "Kinda metro, know what I'm saying? Now this—this is the real funky—" Anthony reached up to touch the vizier's turban. In an instant, two guards were on him, and he was out cold.

Jackie sighed. It seemed that Anthony was spending most of his time in medieval Baghdad unconscious. The vizier glared at her, angry that he'd have to deal with this woman.

"Give us the book," he ordered.

Jackie stumbled backward a step. There was no way she could do that; she and Anthony would be marooned in this time— forever. She knew from past experience that it would lead her home. All she needed to find was the Middle Road as her aunt had told her some time ago. Then she would go through the door to another world—ideally, home.

Tears welled in her eyes once more at what seemed to be a lifetime ago. So much had happened in what was really a short time. So much upheaval and loss—because even though her parents were still alive, they were, in fact, gone. All she wanted was to be back home with them, reading by the fireside, late into the night. With Wolfe curled up at her feet, those were her favorite evenings.

"You will give us the book," the vizier repeated.

Jackie arched a brow. "Are you sure you want to take it?" The vizier frowned at her audacity and motioned for her to set it on a nearby table. As she did so, it seemed to almost breathe. Then the pages began turning on their own, much as they had in the previous room Jackie had shared with Anthony.

"Magnificent," said the vizier. He stepped forward eagerly and reached for the book.

Shahan stayed his arm. "Remember ..."

"Ah, yes," said the vizier excitedly, "but the book speaks to us, even now. Behold!"

Indeed, an outline map appeared before their eyes, and a thin red line snaked across the two pages.

"From the steppes of Central Asia, look, that must be Samarkand, my ancestral home," whispered Shahan. He traced the line as it continued to manifest across the old map. A fierce longing for his childhood land seized his heart. Until the wars, he'd had the best of childhoods, living, as it were, in an oasis of learning and love. How he missed his mother and sisters. *Never mind all that now.* He shook his head. *Praise Allah, that he works in mysterious ways and that I might continue to serve him as best as I know how—in the pursuit of learning and of truth.* Shahan took a deep breath and continued. "That line continues west, straight over the Zagros Mountains, to Baghdad, where we are now."

"Yes, yes, I see all that," the vizier snapped. "I'm no fool. If I were, I'd never be in a position to demand your release—or your head!"

Shahan swallowed hard, thinking of the prison from which he'd recently been freed. The young man continued, the sweat on his upper lip barely concealed by a sparse mustache.

"But this—now, this is unusual." Shahan pointed to three figures that mysteriously appeared in profile, each occupying an extreme corner of the open pages. In the far right upper and lower corners of the right side of the open book, the shadowed profiles of a man and a woman appeared to be reaching toward the empty upper left-hand corner. In the lower left corner of the left page, another dark figure had his back toward them and the illustrations on the open pages. He had his arms up over his face, as if warding off a blow; he seemed to be looking beyond the book at whatever it was that frightened him. Still, that figure appeared to be alternately glowing and fading. The other two figures appeared to be mourning as they reached for an empty space.

Jackie caught her breath, and Shahan eyed her sharply. "You recognize these figures?" he asked softly. He was not entirely unsympathetic to the pretty young woman, who had paled at the sights that appeared before them in the book.

She nodded. Clearly, her parents were reaching out to find her; she should have been in the empty space of the upper left-hand corner. And she could have picked out Devon's bony profile anywhere; it was he who was struggling with an imaginary foe beyond the borders of the page. "But I don't know what all this means," she said softly.

Shahan rubbed his chin, for once not bemoaning the fact that his beard had not fully come in yet. "I know who can help," he said. He thought of two unusual visitors to the House of Wisdom. Clearly, they were traveling scholars, and from their mannerisms, had come from quite a distance. However, the House of Wisdom was open to all scholars who sought to learn, and the sight of exotic visitors in the famous library was nothing new. Curious, he had introduced himself to them, and was struck by their keen grasp of the ancient documents. It wouldn't surprise him if they were invited to assist with the translations.

The vizier shot him a look. "Who?" As his main task was to serve the caliph and handle day-to-day administrative affairs throughout Baghdad, he was not overly familiar with what happened in academic circles.

"There are two traveling scholars from well beyond the borders of Dar al-Islam," Shahan replied. "They have been invited to the House of Wisdom for their understanding of the ancient histories. Indeed, it appears that they are of European descent, and surprisingly, they possess a fair amount of knowledge."

The vizier arched a thick brow. "Really? Why have I not heard of them?" He was displeased. He was supposed to be apprised of all that went on within the caliphate, so that he might best serve the caliph and, naturally, Allah.

"The library director was only recently introduced to them," said Shahan. He hastened to explain further. "He didn't want to bother you with what might turn out to be two imposters. He had to speak to them himself. I know he was about to write you a report on them, because you, O Great Vizier, are renowned for your vigilance in protecting the interests of the Abbasid caliphate."

The vizier didn't respond, and Shahan continued smoothly, with only a slight cough that belied his nervousness. "Indeed, he was wondering if the caliph himself might enjoy their company, but—"

"But that's for me to discern," the vizier growled. "We might as well do that now—and perhaps gain some insight into this situation while we're at it." Shahan nodded, grateful that the vizier still had some use for him. As long as that was the case, he would be able to return to his beloved books. A shadow crossed his face as he thought of the work he'd hidden in his turban. *So much for the quiet life of a scholar,* he thought ruefully.

The vizier interrupted his thoughts. "Well? Shall we find them at the House of Wisdom, even at this hour?"

Shahan nodded. "The library director keeps long hours."

The vizier pressed his lips together. "Not anymore."

Shahan looked at him, surprised, but knew enough to hold his tongue.

"Our director seems to have passed on suddenly." The vizier's face clouded. "A loss beyond words. Clearly, Mohammed's love of learning superseded his human needs. That's how he came to be in charge of the vastest reservoir of knowledge, after all."

He turned to Jackie, who had been following the exchange even as her mind raced with thoughts of her parents. Were they looking for her? Or were they tracking down Devon? Why was Devon turned away from them in the book's images? And why was he frightened?

"Well, the girl must come along, as the book may be handled only by her," said the vizier. "Yet a woman should not enter the House of Wisdom, and certainly has no leave to do so with neither husband nor brother as protection." He glanced down at Anthony and back up again at her. Anthony was still out cold on the floor.

Jackie shook her head; he was neither brother nor husband. She put a hand to her mouth and stifled a giggle. The thought of Anthony as her spouse brought tears of mirth to her eyes.

Shahan and the vizier exchanged glances, appalled by her lack of decorum. "Shocking," the older man muttered under his breath. "You will come with us now," he commanded. He snapped a finger at the guards and barked a quick series of commands.

Moments later, Jackie was given a pile of clothes. "You will wear these and—no!"

Jackie had started to remove the veil from her hair. The men turned away, mortified. "Have you no decency, that you would let any man gaze upon your hair?"

She blushed—of course, she had just read about this in class. *But come on,* she thought angrily, *I'm under a little pressure here!*

She thought back to the day her world history class had discussed typical Muslim garb. One of her classmates, Hani Khan, had enlightened them all. Hani's family had come to Arborville from Pakistan; her father was a professor of Islamic studies at a nearby college. Hers was a devout family of Muslims, and she and her younger sister wore silken hijabs to cover their hair, and long pants and long-sleeved shirts to school every day.

"We believe that it is a sign of respect to cover our hair," she had explained shyly when one of the students asked Ms. Thompson about the connection between covering one's head and faith in a higher power. "In this way, we show that our true devotion is to our family—only our brothers and fathers can see our hair unbound—and to Allah. We are focused on"—and here she chose her words carefully, well aware that she was the only Muslim in the room—"higher matters than our hairstyles. And anyway, it is considered sinful to expose one's hair so that other men might gaze upon it and have dark thoughts." She looked down.

"Can we look at your hair?" Jackie blurted, and then was immediately embarrassed by the silence that followed.

Hani had nodded. "Yes, the girls can." With that, the class erupted in a chorus of pleas by the girls and irritation from the boys.

"So what are *we* supposed to do?" one boy asked.

Ms. Thompson gave the class a grin. "C'mon, boys." She ushered all the males in the classroom out the door. "This will take only a second." She nodded to a fellow teacher on hall duty just outside her classroom. "If any of them make a peep, I'll—"

Anthony had held up a hand. "For a beautiful woman like you, don't worry, I got it covered, Ms. Thompson." The class groaned; he'd made no secret of his crush on the lovely teacher.

Ms. Thompson looked at him seriously. "Thank you, Anthony." Then she pushed the last of the boys out into the hallway, locked the classroom door, and quickly taped a poster over the small window in the door.

Hani unpinned her hijab, and let her long black hair unfurl below her waist. The girls in the class gasped. Lustrous, jet black, and silken, Hani's hair seemed to have a life of its own.

"It's so … beautiful," one girl murmured. "Can we touch it?" Hani nodded.

It was not lost on the girls that Hani's whole face was transformed by the thick, dark hair that framed it. "So soft …," the girls whispered. "Wow, incredible." Her hair seemed all the more beautiful for having never been seen. "I can't believe it."

"I can see why you'd want to keep your hair under wraps," Ms. Thompson acknowledged. "It really is quite alluring."

"Yes, and the only man not in my family who will see it shall be my husband," Hani replied shyly, winding her hair back up and tucking it into her hijab.

Just in time, too, for there was an insistent rapping at the door. "Sorry, Ms. Thompson," Anthony shouted through the door. "I tried to hold him back, but the principal wants to know what's going on."

In fact, the principal had obtained a key from a nearby custodian and unlocked the door himself, outraged that a female student was "revealing herself" in the classroom, as one of the boys had said, snickering. Ms. Thompson let Hani do all the talking, and by the time she was finished, she had invited everyone in the class, as well as the principal, to be guests at a local prayer service the next Friday. "Our holy day," she'd explained. Jackie smiled at the memory.

The men had left Jackie to dress, deciding that an unconscious Anthony couldn't cause any harm. Her fingers shaking, Jackie twisted her hair up and, with great difficulty, wrapped the turban around her head, tucking the loose end into a fold near the crown. She adjusted the robe around her body and tied the cloth belt securely. With a glance at Anthony, who'd been lifted onto surrounding cushions and was now snoring loudly, she stepped outside the small chamber, Aunt Isobel's book clutched to her chest. The turban slid down, nearly blocking her vision.

The vizier snorted, and even Shahan failed to hide a smile.

"Come, my beardless scholar," he said. "Let us see what treasures can be discovered in the House of Wisdom."

There was a door to which I found no key; there was a veil through which I could not see.
—Omar Khayyam

Chapter XIV

Message from Beyond

As the sun was making its slow descent over the bustling city by the Tigris, its inhabitants noted its westward arc through the cloudless sky and picked up their pace. The worst heat of the day had passed, and now a second round of activities marked the time. Where the tailor accepted work in the morning, now he was ready to hand over new and mended clothes. A young boy scurried to the marketplace, spurred on by the urgency in his mother's voice. She had run out of cardamom—woe! The evening meal would not be complete without this essential spice. The boy ran up to the spice seller, eyes rounding as his gaze lingered on the beautiful, colorful mounds of spices, aromas mingling in the open air. As the flurry of the market swirled around him, the boy stood rooted in front of the display, grounded for a short moment. He breathed in deeply, luxuriating in the riches before him. Then he made his purchase and took flight, his small, dirty heels kicking up hot dust in his wake.

In a dark corner of an alley off the marketplace, a stranger leaned against a low-lying, shuttered house. This alley had once been called the Avenue of Alchemists—a joke, of course, as it was barely a person wide—but no one came down it anymore. Still, it was said that all sorts of forbidden activity brewed, away from the open gaze of the rare passerby.

The stranger turned his gaze down the alley, which was all quiet, save for a clanging that thrummed with an unnatural vibration. Devon smiled. He could feel the energy curling around his ankles and working its way up. *Good. It was working.*

The sound spilled out of the alley and into the marketplace, where it was lost in a chorus of harangues and exchange, praises to Allah, and the general din of humanity gathering in the timeless exchange of buying, selling, and the sharing of goods, services, knowledge, and faith.

* * *

Jackie's feet barely touched the ground as she was escorted across the main courtyard of the House of Wisdom between the vizier and Shahan, a full phalanx of guards right on their heels. There was no way to go but forward, and they were moving fast. The vizier absolutely did not want to be stopped and hailed, because, as he put it, "That would entail precious time wasted in theoretical chatter."

Shahan had flinched at those words, in part because there were, in fact, days—not to mention weeks—where all real study would cease as the scholars pored over a particular piece and argued about what should be translated, and how. There were those who believed that any and all spiritual work of the ancients should be discarded at once, as the Greeks and Romans were polytheistic; to preserve such nonsense would be a direct affront to Allah. They argued that only scientific and mathematical works should be preserved.

"But what of work that references their many gods?" Shahan had asked one of his mentors.

"Discard it," came the curt reply. "It is disrespectful, and knowledge that is grounded in those kinds of beliefs cannot be real knowledge, after all." That set off a firestorm of a debate as other scholars argued that this was surely the way to eliminate much ancient learning, as nearly all the works had some sort of allusion to Greek or Roman gods. Some scholars argued that they had the right to alter the material to preserve its original scholarly intent but frame it better within the context of Islam. One such translator substituted the word *Allah* for *Zeus*. "Are these not essentially the same?" he asked. "And did not even the concept of a Zeus truly originate with Allah, who has made all things and created all ideas?"

Shahan had come to trust his own judgment in these matters, and as his reputation as a translator had grown, he had become bolder. Fully fluent in Greek, Latin, Aramaic, and Persian, he used the power of these languages to find deeper truths within the scripts, truths that would resonate with his Arabic audience, indeed all of Dar al-Islam.

But all this took time. Lots of it. And it was easy to be dragged into side conversations on existence, meaning, and faith, even as the scholars pored over the work before them. As he escorted his small party to the inner sanctum of the scholars in the House of Wisdom, Shahan's anxiety doubled. What was the vizier planning to do? His fears were not allayed when he saw two strangers examining a document with his old mentor, Achmed. They had turned slightly away from the other scholars in a subtle attempt at privacy.

Light filtered down upon Achmed and the visitors from keyhole windows high up on the wall, bathing the room in a serene glow. They sat barefoot on a large dark blue Persian carpet that filled most of the entire room, its knotted fringe overlapping a smaller rug of a lighter hue. A bundle of scrolls had been carefully placed to the side, and apart from a pile of cushions, there were no other objects in the smallish study room. The smaller of the two visitors, slight as a boy, straightened, furrowing his brow. The scholar looked up, and Shahan staggered back in shock. The small scholar looked remarkably like the young woman he'd just smuggled in. Shahan saw them lock eyes, and caught Jackie just as she passed out.

"Out! Everyone out!" screamed the vizier, and the room cleared of scholars, translators, and scribes. "There, I think he's coming to …" He frowned. "Now get him up, and quick!"

The others stared at him, surprised by his harshness. *Why the rush?* Shahan wondered. Then he glanced down and understood; the girl's turban had started to come undone. Allah forbid it was discovered that a young girl—a woman, even—had been smuggled into the House of Wisdom—and not in the company of her brothers, father, or husband.

Through the dark fringes of her lashes, the images before Jackie slowly began to come into focus. The young scholar, Shahan; the vizier; and three strangers peered down at her with not a little concern. She took a deep breath, willing herself into another place. *Can't this all be a dream?* she pleaded with no one in particular. Then she felt a familiar burning sensation: the book from Samarkand. *I might as well get this over with,* she thought. Not quite trusting her voice, she opened her eyes and looked around. She looked again at the strange scholars, and a wave of dizziness and nausea threatened her consciousness once more.

Her parents were in the room with her.

"I think this one will be fine, praise Allah," said her father.

"Yes, indeed. He is most merciful," her mother said, nodding.

Jackie passed out again.

Knowledge is the conformity of the object and the intellect.
—Ibn Rushd

Chapter XV

An Extra Dimension

WHEN JACKIE CAME TO, SHE was propped up on a pile of cushions. Shahan wordlessly offered her a steaming cup of tea. Then he slid his eyes to the vizier, who was deep in discussion with the two strange scholars and Achmed.

"Yes, a series of most interesting events indeed," said the vizier, pulling on his straggling beard. He did this when he was puzzled, which didn't happen too often. He had a sharp mind, and was quite unused to being stumped. "*Ey!*" He winced, and shook a few loose hairs from his hand. When he was really upset, the vizier would pluck out his beard; the pain forced him to action.

"You see," said David Tempo, "we believe that one of our own, from the northern countries, has acquired one of the Ur-texts from Samarkand, not unlike the one held by that one on the cushions." Jackie stared at her father, mute. He held her gaze. *Steady,* he seemed to say. *Not a word.*

"Perhaps I should execute them both," the vizier pondered. David Tempo suppressed a shudder and exchanged glances with his wife, who nodded slightly. They knew the risks.

Jackie felt a surge of blinding anger, and then the shock of fear. Here were her parents—finally!—but pretending that nothing was amiss. *Sure, let's just risk our lives in other dimensions for fun. I'm a pawn once again,* she thought bitterly. *Just bait to lure Devon back to where he belongs; I've always been a good girl.* But she knew better: Devon was actively pursuing that which could alter the course of the world. In an instant, she was ashamed of herself. Her parents had no choice. Of course, neither did she.

Her father gave a slight cough as he started to explain. "You see, O Great Vizier, these particular books were crafted by a supreme possessor of knowledge and were unearthed by a most worthy scholar and kept for safekeeping by one who could be trusted."

"Yes, yes, I can see that they are special, but so are all these documents." The vizier waved a hand at the tables scattered with rolls. "Indeed, these contain the most valuable of information, from profound mathematical principles to scientific observations on astrological principles." He glowered at Jackie. "I know not what strange magic your book possesses, but it is almost certainly not sanctioned by the principles that govern Dar al-Islam. However, if one such tome falls into the wrong hands …" His voice drifted off. "It is quite a challenge to imagine that a European," he said with a trace of contempt, "can pose a threat to the great Abbasid dynasty."

"Any one person can do just that, and worse," Judith Tempo pitched her voice low to conceal her gender; revealing that she was a woman could prove fatal. She glanced at her daughter, pleading for her forgiveness. *This is why we're here, pumpkin,* Jackie read in her eyes. The teen ducked her head, unwilling to betray her welling emotion.

"But how—"

"Sire! You're wanted!" A guard ran breathlessly into the room, mindful not to stare directly at the vizier or his guests. "So sorry, sire, it's an emergency." He kept his gaze respectfully lowered.

With a great sigh of annoyance, the vizier threw up his hands. "As to be expected. Very well," he said. Then he turned to the small group assembled around the table, with Jackie's book now in front of them. "You will stay here," he ordered, and nodded at the guard, who stepped outside the chamber to keep watch. "I will summon the assistant director, so that we might have access to what we need." Pulling his robe tightly around himself, in spite of the midday heat, the vizier tucked his chin and marched decisively out the door to handle any situation that might challenge the caliph—and, by extension, the Abbasid dynasty.

The small group was quiet for a few moments. Then Achmed stood, hand firmly on Shahan's shoulder. "Well, my son, I think it would be right for some more tea to be served at this hour, *neh?*" He stretched, glancing at the documents scattered on nearby tables. "They won't be coming back anytime soon," he said, meaning the translators and scholars. "I will order the tea myself. The assistant director will most likely arrive after early-evening prayers, and he would want refreshments."

"But the vizier—" Shahan started to protest. They weren't supposed to leave the room.

Achmed smiled and brought a finger to his lips. Though his eyes twinkled, Jackie felt cold: there was a strange darkness behind the levity of his gaze. She shivered.

"I'll be back," Achmed said, and he stepped neatly through a secret doorway that none of them, not even Shahan, had noticed. They saw that the steps were leading down, and the old scholar shut the door firmly behind him.

Shahan shook his head, wondering at the mysteries of the House of Wisdom. Clearly there were well-kept secrets hidden right before his eyes. He had been studying at the most famous library in Baghdad for nearly six months now and had never noticed the secret passageway before. He sighed and turned his attention to the visitors before him.

His eyes narrowed as he considered the three, two of whom were ill fitted with scholars' robes and turbans. They were all unnaturally pale. The smaller ones closely resembled each other, each with a smattering of light freckles, light green eyes flecked with gold, and delicate bone structure. They could be twins, he mused, chin in hand, but for the fact that they were clearly more than a few years apart. Shahan noticed that they were watching him closely as well; they were very still, he saw, as if they were waiting for something.

"By Allah!" Shahan pushed back from the table with a sudden haste. He knew what had been bothering him and stared at each of the strangers in turn. "You—you are all related!" He looked from Jackie to her mother and back again. "Are you a woman, then, as well?" His head was spinning, but he knew better than to call in the guard—he had his own secrets that needed safekeeping. The older woman paled further, if that was possible. Her tiny freckles stood out even more clearly, and her pupils dilated with fear. But she remained calm. Shahan pressed on. "Are you ... her sister or, perhaps, her mother?"

The woman remained seated. "Yes. We are related. I am her mother." Her voice was tightly controlled, even as her eyes filled with tears. She looked up at her tall companion.

"And I am her father," the man added. "My given name is David Tempo, and this is my wife, Judith." He had stood up at Shahan's abrupt behavior. The Muslim scholar could see now that his was a defensive posture; the tall, angular man was ready to protect his family with his life, if need be.

The secret door swung open into the room, and a slave boy walked in, bearing a tray of tea. No one spoke as the quiet child set the tray before them. Shahan motioned the child away. "I will serve them myself," he said when the boy made to pour the drink. The boy disappeared on Shahan's orders, taking care to shut the door behind himself.

Shahan poured the steaming liquid into four ceramic cups, which he did not pass out. Jackie looked at him inquiringly. Why bother going through the motions if—?

"It is highly unusual for drink to be served in this room, among so many ancient documents, including the book you possess," Shahan said quietly. "Please. Tell me where you are really from, and what you have come seeking."

Judith clasped her daughter's hand, and closed her eyes. "It is true that we are tracking down one of our own kind. He has stolen a book like the one in my daughter's possession."

Jackie glanced up at her father. "His uncle," she said, indicating Shahan, "had a similar book stolen from his library."

Judith opened her eyes and looked at the Muslim scholar. "Well, then, we are victims of the same criminal. "

David set his own book from ancient Samarkand on the table next to Jackie's. Both books began to glow with an unnatural light.

"These ancient books," Judith said, "and one more that Devon—that's his name—stole from us, appeared in my father's bookstore one day when I was but a young girl." She explained how a wooden crated box had mysteriously appeared on the steps of her father's bookstore, and how she and her sister, Isobel, discovered that these were no ordinary tomes.

"Though all books have the power to transport their readers to another time and place," Judith continued, "*these* books are literally capable of doing so." She talked of how she and her sister had realized the power of the books when they found themselves going back in time, with the power to return at will—or more accurately, when the books sensed that they should return home. Their adventures became quite risky, however, and the girls had vowed not to touch the books further.

"As the years went by, we ignored their call," said Judith. "This was easier to do when the books were split up. So two of the books were stored at our home and the third in my sister's library."

David picked up the story. "Then Devon showed up. He tracked me down—I'm a professor, and he was my student—suspecting, quite rightly, that I had at least one of these special volumes. He stole one from my very own collection of books."

Shahan frowned sharply. "An abominable act for one who aspires to be a scholar," he said.

The Tempos exchanged glances. "If you could say that was his goal," David said. He laughed softly, and not without a hint of bitterness.

"So my parents have been pursuing him ever since," Jackie interjected, and Shahan shifted his gaze to the turbaned girl. "In China, in the fifteen hundreds; in eighteenth-century Brazil; here …"

"I am not familiar with this land of Brazil," Shahan said, "but there is something you should know."

Their quiet discussion was interrupted by the muezzin's prayer, and his call to respect the glory of Allah rang over all of Baghdad from the highest of towers. Shahan got up, unrolled his prayer mat in the direction of Mecca, and prepared to pray. All of Baghdad had come to a halt, and a hush descended upon the marvelous city. For many, the last prayer of the day would take place in the privacy of their homes.

"Allahu Akbar!" Shahan raised his hands. "God is great!" Then he folded his hands over his chest and began to recite from the Qur'an. The Tempos waited, curious but respectful, as Shahan alternately stood, bowed, and prostrated himself on his prayer mat. "Peace be with you, and God's blessings," Shahan said to the family, completing his prayers.

"And also with you," Jackie replied without missing a beat, surprising herself. It had been a long time since she had prayed. Her father put his arm around her and gave her shoulders a squeeze.

"There is a fourth book," Shahan told them, rolling up his mat once prayers were over. "Can you tell me where that one is?"

"That's impossible! Four?" Judith was visibly shocked.

Shahan nodded. "As the ancients so determined. When I was quite young, my tutor explained that according to such wisdom, there are four cardinal directions: north, south, east, and west. This, of course, we accept as common knowledge. And four elements: earth, wind, fire, and water. The four fluids of the body, which the Greeks believed affected temperament: blood, phlegm, bile, and choler. And the physical universe is composed of these four: matter, time, space, and energy."

"And four dimensions," added David. He looked at his daughter. "You know this," he said.

Jackie nodded, righting her turban, which was sliding down her face again. "Yes—a single point, a flat plane, and a cube—all of which represent the first three dimensions. The fourth is time, the passage of which we experience." She gave her parents a rueful smile. "Remember when I first asked about that?"

Judith smiled at the memory. "You were eight years old and reading *A Wrinkle in Time*," she said. "That's when we decided to tell you about the … books." She turned to Shahan, who had been following this exchange quite closely. "We thought there were only three books that could take the reader back in time. Each one has a way out for the reader to return home—to his or her original starting point." She pointed at the two books on the table. "Look!"

Shahan took a deep breath as both books radiated extra warmth; it seemed even the table began to grow warm. The patterns on the book covers glowed and swirled.

Just then, the guard poked his head into the room and scowled as he checked to see that they were all still there. All conversation ceased until he was gone.

David said to no one in particular as he paced around the room, "We had no knowledge of its existence before this. I wonder if this fourth book is different from the others."

Shahan nodded. "It is." Jackie's father stopped to stare at him.

"So what does the book do?" Jackie asked.

The young scholar paused, wondering whether to divulge this long-held secret. He decided to take the plunge.

"The fourth book takes the reader far beyond his point of origin—and well into the future."

Teach thy tongue to say "I do not know," and thou shalt progress.
—Maimonides

Chapter XVI

A Last Supper

Arborville, present time

"Thank you. That was delicious," Jon said. He wiped his mouth with an ivory linen napkin and sat back, ready to excuse himself from the table.

"Young man." Aunt Isobel peered sternly over her wire-rimmed spectacles. "You hardly touched your meal." She dropped her hands onto her lap and leaned forward, peering intently into his pale face. "Come, now."

It was true. Jon looked down at his plate. He had consumed only half of his chicken teriyaki, and he had ignored the tempura vegetables, though he normally loved the crunch of the batter-fried carrots and broccoli.

"I'm sorry." He picked up his fork and set it down again, restless. Then he ran a hand through his shaggy dark hair. "I know that this will all turn out fine." He fixed his gaze on the enormous, multitiered crystal chandelier that hung low over the long teak dining table. Light refracted off each individual cut droplet, radiating brightness and shine throughout the room. *Why was I left behind this time?* He thought of the last time Jackie had opened Aunt Isobel's book, only to discover that she had been sent back to the most horrific place imaginable. He shuddered, thinking of her early adventures in eighteenth-century Brazil as she tried to rescue her mother, who was imprisoned in the jungle. Jon couldn't travel back in time with her then, as his own mother was near death, but now … He shook his head, willing the whole situation away.

Aunt Isobel fixed a keen eye on the shaken young man. "It's not easy to be close to someone who keeps disappearing, is it?" she said softly.

Jon started; she had read his mind.

"I thought so," the short, white-haired woman said, not unkindly. Her amethyst-colored eyes shone sympathetically. "Rare is the fellow who knows that a girl must find her own way."

It suddenly occurred to Jon that Isobel L'eroux must have lost her own great love. As far as he or anyone in the small town of Arborville knew, she had never been married. She did travel quite a bit, for her line of work—the acquisition and sale of classical art and antiques—necessarily entailed being the first to get the scoop on goods, even before they came on the market. She was enormously wealthy, though why she lived in a mansion as large and as lavish as Shangri-la was beyond him. With only Dona Marta, the Brazilian housekeeper, and James, the butler, to keep her company, it was as if she had a grand hotel to herself—and almost as if she were waiting for a large party to arrive.

"Who—," Jon began, but Isobel put a finger to her lips.

"Not important. Come," she said as she got up. When he stood as well, she took his arm, steering him to the library, which was just off the dining room. Isobel had designed the house herself, and details such as these—the flow of rooms—had been important. "The library is always the perfect place to retire after a meal," she liked to say.

Dona Marta came in to clear the table, muttering to herself. "*Nossa Senhora*—the Virgin Mary—what a waste!" She tucked an inky lock of hair behind her ear and was finished in an instant.

It wasn't hard, what with only two guests for dinner. "I thought I was cooking for four, and only half the company showed up!" Ah well, she'd keep a plate for Jackie, who would need dinner at some point.

In the next room, Aunt Isobel stood with her young guest in her richly stocked library. *There must be at least five hundred books here,* Jon thought, not for the first time. It was one of his favorite places to visit. Aunt Isobel brushed a few dog hairs off her simple silk kimono and tightened its wide sash about her waist. *And she must have at least that many outfits,* he thought fondly; tracking down exotic fashion was yet another one of her many creative pursuits.

"I have some paperwork to prepare for my next voyage abroad." Isobel patted the teen's arm, looking directly into his dark eyes. He tried to hunch down a bit as she tilted her chin up at a sharp angle. "She will be fine. They will all be fine. James will see you out when you're ready to leave."

Jon thanked her and sat down, wondering what on earth he should—or could—do next. James had stoked a roaring fire, and Jon sank into the wonderful warmth of a plush velour couch across from it. He leaned his head back, then grabbed a decorative throw pillow and toyed with its tassels. *Where is she now?* he wondered as he traced the pattern of the fabric with his eyes until he grew dizzy from the effort. He closed his eyes, the interlocking red-and-gold design seared into his mind, repeating over and over until it blocked all else.

Wolfe had trotted into the room with him earlier, and the great dog nudged him now, whining softly. He missed Jackie. Jon let a hand drop and rest on the dog's head, stroking him gently. "I miss her, too, big guy," he said. Wolfe settled at his feet with a grunt, and Jon sank more deeply into the couch. Lulled by the warmth, conscious only of the softness of the cushions, Jon slipped into an uneasy slumber, unsure of what was real, what was imagined, and what was yet to come.

* * *

Jon awoke with a start, to find that the large dog had clambered up on the couch with him and burrowed deep into his side. He pushed the dog aside and sat up slowly, thick with sleep. The fire was nearly out now, and Jon shivered, disoriented and not a little cold.

Now he knew what was bothering him: something about Jackie's backpack. He remembered that she was missing a book that was critical to her project with Anthony. She had checked it out from the library at school, and it had somehow disappeared. He picked up the backpack, which stood nearby. It was already unzipped. Strange … It smelled of sandalwood and ashes, not scents he associated with her at all. A little self-conscious, he flipped through the books and papers—nothing. The reference book on Islamic culture wasn't there. But then he found the source of the exotic scents.

"What the—?" Jon fished out what was clearly a man's linen handkerchief. He raised it carefully and studied it with suspicion. It was very well made, ivory shot through with threads of gold in a strangely familiar pattern. The letter *D* was monogrammed in one of the corners.

"*D* is for … dammit—and deception!" Pushed to the edge by the events of the day, Jon was angry and disbelieving. What was Jackie doing with another man's possession? And who was this "D"? Jon walked over to the library's French doors and stared out into the inky darkness. He knew that far, far below, the Atlantic Ocean roiled like his emotions, crashing against the stony New England beach at the bottom of the cliffs. He thought of the familiar saying "I'm in a relationship—and it's complicated." Well, no one could top the fact that he was involved with a time traveler in search of her parents—or so she claimed. Maybe she was really cheating on him. He sighed; he knew what he saw—and what he'd experienced, having crossed over to China with her not long ago. Still, he couldn't help but feel a surge of suspicion. What was she doing at this very moment? He didn't know what to think anymore, and this was not a feeling he wanted to deal with, not now or maybe ever. Jon balled up his fists in anger and frustration—and not a little bit of fear. Maybe Jackie was in trouble after all. And maybe there was nothing he could do about it.

"Damn!" He ran a hand though his thick dark hair. He needed to get a copy of the missing reference book; that might help him track her down. Then he stared at the cloth in his other hand. He crumpled it up and stuffed it deep into his pocket. And then he pushed open the French doors and leaned into the wind, heedless of the building fury of the oncoming storm.

Two truths cannot contradict each other.
—Ibn Rushd

Chapter XVII

Life Everlasting

Baghdad, 927 CE

"WELL?"

The alchemist looked up at the speaker, a strange, fair-haired patron who had generously funded his latest projects. But the man did not seem to appreciate that there was a specific method to the procedure he was asking of him now—indeed, of all procedures—and that if rushed, the results could be disastrous.

The alchemist sighed. Most people wanted him to perform silly tricks—silly to him at least—such as changing copper into gold, water into wine. He'd tried to patiently explain to would-be customers that that was not the true purpose of alchemy. No: his science was one of real, meaningful transformation, and in this sense, it respected both the laws of science and those of Allah.

This was exactly the problem now, however. This foreigner wanted to tamper with the most basic forces of the universe: life and death! The alchemist drew a breath as he worked, checking the ancient formulas to be sure. Any false move, any mistake, would result in real disaster—not just for his client, but perhaps the entire city and beyond.

"I asked you a question!" A pale fist came crashing down on a makeshift table in the corner of the room where the stranger lurked. "When will you be finished?"

A small glass vial rolled across the table and stopped precipitously at the edge. The alchemist kept his eyes focused on the small object as he answered the stranger in measured tones.

"The procedure will be complete … when all the proper steps have been taken and all instructions followed in the manner described and in accordance with the laws of …" The alchemist watched as the vial shattered on the cold stone floor. *There will be more destruction to follow,* he thought with more than a little apprehension. Not for the first time, his mind turned to what had led him to accept the stranger's offer.

It seemed so long ago that he had been introduced to the shifty-looking foreigner by an esteemed scholar from the House of Wisdom. The scholar had long been a regular customer who often came into his shop seeking this or that potion to strengthen his mind for the vigorous studies demanded of him. Often he would supply the alchemist with his own formulas and watch as the alchemist combined the ingredients himself. Then he would down the murky results in a gulp, smacking his lips and declaring himself ready for another round with the works of Aristotle.

"Now my mind is clear, my friend! Not only am I ready to translate and decipher the works of the ancients, but I can see through to their real meaning and to the beginning of time, to our real purpose here, praise Allah!" The scholar's eyes would take on an unnatural gleam within minutes of consuming the potion.

The alchemist was uncomfortable with the scholar's invocation of the highest power, but the man was in the service of the most venerated learning palace, and therefore he had to respect him. After all, one did not get so close to Truth without being worthy of the task, he reasoned.

Still, the scholar was a regular customer, to the point where he demanded exclusive patronage of the alchemist's laboratory.

"I will be your patron, my friend," the scholar had declared last month, and tossed him a bag of dinars, "and you will have no other." The alchemist quickly agreed, as the bag contained a very handsome salary, more than enough to cover the cost of having two wives and six children. If he wanted another wife, he'd have to be able to fund her expenses as well.

The alchemist was relatively content to take care of the scholar's strange habits, though there were times when the man would act even more eccentric than usual after taking his strange potions. He would lurch around the room, laugh wildly, and speak to voices that he alone could hear.

Last week, however, the scholar had brought a pale, strange-looking visitor, a weasel-like man with golden, translucent hair that straggled from his dark turban. The foreigner strode into the makeshift laboratory with the assurance of an emperor. "So, Achmed, this is the place," he said, and gave a curt nod to the alchemist.

As Achmed bowed in the affirmative, the alchemist noted his patron's discomfort. Achmed twitched slightly, tugged at his turban, and then tried to appear pensive by scratching his straggly beard. He looked as if he hadn't slept much over the past few days. Finally, he settled down, staring at a stain on the floor as the foreigner wandered about the secret laboratory.

"Ha! You need to stay focused, my friend," said the odd-looking stranger, clapping a thin hand on the scholar's shoulder. "The fate of the *world* is at stake!"

The alchemist, bent over his work, was startled at such familiarity. He knew that he was to keep to his work, such as it was. Achmed had made clear that he was to talk to no one of his work, and thus it was not his place to join in the discussion, not even with a traditional offering of tea. Yet who was the foreigner to treat the great scholar Achmed with such a lack of respect? Was he not familiar with Achmed's translations of Aristotle's political discourse? The alchemist felt his pulse quicken at such disrespect.

But the stranger continued: "Trust me, when the formula is complete, you'll have no need of your own ... special tonics to help you see The Way. You'll know everything, and more. You will be the most brilliant scholar in all of Baghdad, for you will possess a wisdom and a clarity with which no one can compete. And as we both know"—the stranger's voice took on low, hypnotic tones as he gazed into the scholar's eyes—"true knowledge is the key to immortality."

The alchemist had held his breath at such blasphemy, for who was the stranger to make such declarations? As far as he could tell, the man was not one of the faithful; perhaps he had *dhimmi* status, and as such was either Jewish or Christian, the People of the Book. But given the way the stranger went on about the kingdom of heaven and the true nature of existence, he doubted very much that the man followed any faith at all.

The scholar Achmed paced the small room furiously and then turned on the alchemist, irritated that he would not be imbibing any of his thinking potions, as he liked to call them. To show any possible weakness in front of the stranger would be unthinkable. Sweat beaded on his forehead, and his eyes bulged slightly. "Follow the formula!" he barked at the alchemist, and threw another bag of coins on the laboratory table. Then he and the stranger strode out, leaving the man with an impossible task—and the impossible lure of immense wealth.

A few days later, the alchemist was still hard at work in his lab, and Devon—as the stranger was called—lurked in the cramped room most of the day. Achmed was nowhere to be found, and Devon's presence was unsettling, to say the least. On occasion, he'd lounge about out in the alley, making sure that all was quiet. As per his instructions, Achmed had sealed the narrow street; it was his property, anyway, and he could do as he wished. A few gold coins slipped to the magistrate had ensured that it would be so—but only for a week.

Now Achmed's "friend" hovered over the alchemist's work. He made his impatience clear. "Hurry up, you tedious man!" Devon snarled.

The alchemist refrained from making a sharp retort; there was something quite sinister about the man, and he had a large family to tend. "As I said before, I must follow the instructions to their exact specifications."

Devon turned on his heel, his dusty robe whirling as he stalked out into the alley. A few minutes later, he returned, a thick volume in hand.

"Look, you fool!" The foreigner thumped the book down and began riffling through the pages filled with strange symbols and—Allah forbid!—images of humans at work and at play. The alchemist averted his eyes, for it was against divine law for the human form to be reproduced as such. Only Allah could create that which was human.

"This is the result—don't you see?"

Then the alchemist gasped and staggered back at the strange scene before him. He gaped at Devon, nodding dumbly.

"So get back to work!" Devon slammed the book shut.

The alchemist obeyed, trembling. What he had just seen was beyond imagination. Was it not wrong? Or maybe he was following divine orders; perhaps he doubted the path, as had so many holy prophets who could see into the future. He glanced at the heavy bag of coins on his laboratory table. These had come just in time to pay his rent and feed his large family. Yes, faith would see him through. There was a reason why Achmed and now Devon had found their way to his lab. Only true scholars had access to the Truth. He had a higher purpose, the alchemist told himself, and set the dinars aside.

Still, he could not help but fear for his immortal soul. He shook his head and went back to work.

The risk of a wrong decision is preferable to the terror of indecision.
—Maimonides

Chapter XVIII

Library Secrets

Arborville High School, present time

THE FIRST FINGERS OF EARLY-MORNING light reached deep into the recesses of the high school library, sliding across the lustrous marble floor, up and over the tables, and into the dark stacks, where hundreds of books awaited the touch of a curious reader. It was in this state of semidarkness that Jon slowly pushed open the heavy glass door.

Technically, he wasn't supposed to be in the grand room, let alone the building—not just yet. *Not at this ungodly hour,* Jon thought, though he knew full well he was invited to explore the vast library any time he wished.

He thought back to the first time he had been allowed to check out a book from the high school library—what an adventure! Upset at his parents' bitter fights at home, aware of their impending divorce, and unwilling to back down in front of bullies who ate vulnerability for lunch, he had been getting into fights nearly every recess period in middle school. Finally, his seventh-grade English teacher, Mrs. Reeves, marched him across the small junior-senior high school campus and into the high school library.

Mrs. Reeves knew full well that a good book would stop Jon in his tracks. She had seen him in the hallways, book open, frozen but for the shoves of irritated schoolmates who tried to push him out of their way. And indeed, the day he walked into the high school library changed everything for him.

Mrs. Reeves and Mrs. Housel were good friends, and clearly they were collaborators when it came to pushing students beyond their perceived boundaries.

"Mrs. Housel," said his teacher, "here's the young man I mentioned. With your permission, we'd like to introduce him to the high school library."

The petite librarian smiled at the scarecrow of a boy whose eyes seemed almost too big for his face as he absorbed his surroundings. Jon had stood gaping at the vast collection as his future at the high school library was discussed.

"My pleasure," said Mrs. Housel, smiling. "Allow me." As she gave him a tour of the great room, she was impressed by his quiet self-confidence. Most middle-school boys would be mortified talking books with a librarian. Instead, this clear-eyed young man, already taller than she was, didn't want anything more from her than to be able to explore books as he saw fit.

She was also pleased that Jon respected the newly constructed space; when he picked up a crumpled paper on the floor, his actions cemented her conviction that he should be able to stay. From then on, Jon was allowed free access to the library's collection, and in return, she put him to work shelving books as needed. When he wasn't outside running track or cross-country, he could be found among the stacks, searching for the next great book, an escape from the pressures and pull of the outside world.

As Jon slung his backpack on the table now, five years later, he grinned at the memory of the first book he had checked out: *Grendel,* by John Gardner. He hadn't wanted to admit to Mrs. Housel that he was more than a little intimidated by the enormous collection of books. Where to begin? On impulse, he had pulled a thin volume from the stacks: on the cover was a highly detailed pencil sketch of a hideous monster cradling a human skull. Perfect!

"Are you sure?" Mrs. Housel tried to hide her smile. "It's a bit ... dark."

Jon was sure, and a few years later he surprised his tenth-grade teacher by defending the monster's point of view as they discussed *Beowulf.*

"Grendel was lonely, and he really had no choice—it was him against the world," he'd explained to his teacher while the class stared in shock. Fortunately, his teacher was interested, and he later showed her Gardner's book.

"The best part about teaching," she'd remarked, "is learning from my students." She gave him a quick hug and then buried herself in the book.

Grendel against the world ... or rather, me against the world. Jon pushed the thought down in an attempt to avoid a bout of self-pity. His had been a rough adolescence, what with his parents' divorce and later, his mother's illness. Books and running had provided numbing escapes; he often read until he passed out late at night, bone weary from tough workouts. Now that the worst was over, though, the library comforted him like an old friend.

He hoped this old friend would help him now, as he strained to think of how best to help Jackie and Anthony. They had the book from Samarkand that had transported them back in time, it was true, but somehow Jon knew that an answer could be found here. An image grazed the edge of his consciousness—there it was! He shook his head and tried to focus, but then gave up on reason.

As he slowly walked through the brightening library, Jon felt a thrumming in his temples. His hands grazed the tables, chairs, and books, and he felt pulled to the unknown, to that which was unbidden but beckoned nonetheless. As he walked deeper into the library, still dark in these rarely used stacks, he was unable—unwilling?—to turn back into the light. From far, far away, he could hear a door creak slowly open—and swing shut.

Footsteps echoed down the length of the library, and the bank of lights overhead came on one by one. The computers hummed to life, far behind him now.

He had come to the end of the library and stood facing a blank plaster wall. *I don't remember this.* Jon frowned. He turned: behind him stood the large columns, and to each side, row upon row of stacks. He had thought the back wall was lined with books and a few quiet reading desks, but apparently not. There was about two feet between the last stack and the plaster wall.

Why even bother? Jon wondered; it was nearly impossible to crouch down and see the titles. It was not like Mrs. Housel to hide books. And the wall—unfinished plaster, so out of keeping with the rest of the magnificent library. Jon moved behind the stack to his right, tapped the wall, and was immediately showered with pale flakes.

"Ugh!" He spat.

Then all at once, the wall seemed to shift. Jon tried to step back but was right up against the stack of books, cold spines pressing into his back. The outline of a large circle shimmered through. It looked like a human-sized compass. Jon rubbed his eyes. *Now I'm really losing it,* he thought. He leaned forward to take a look, and the circle—a portal of sorts, he could see that now—swung open and away, heavy as a medieval castle door, creaking noisily on ancient hinges.

Jon pushed the door open a bit more, ducked, and walked through.

Mrs. Housel missed him by seconds.

"Gordon," she sighed. She had seen Jon pass through the door, which vanished in the blink of an eye. Now the wall was as before—blank and opaque. "Oh, Gordon, now what have you done?"

You must accept the truth from whatever source it comes.
—Maimonides

Chapter XIX

Prophet and Prayer

Baghdad, 927 CE

THE MUEZZIN'S LAST CALL TO prayers rang out through the darkness as the city prepared to finally turn in. The Tempos watched as Shahan unrolled his prayer mat for the last time that day; they bowed their head in respect, each thinking of what had happened and what was meant to be. The vizier and his entourage had not yet returned, but that didn't mean they were free to go; guards were posted just outside the door.

Dear ... anyone, Jackie thought fervently, head down, blinking back fierce tears, *please help us find a way.* It was hard for her to be more specific: where to start? *Anyone who's listening, help us find our way back home. All of us.* She glanced at her parents, who were also lost in thought. With a guilty start, she thought of Anthony, still back at the harem or, more likely, in some terrible prison. *Help us save Anthony. Help us stop Devon. Help us make things go right.*

Her grandmother, a devout Catholic, had tried to instill in Jackie the enormous power of prayer. "Ask, and ye shall receive; seek, and ye shall find." But ever since she was a child, Jackie had

had trouble praying for herself—or even for her family. "We don't really need anything, Nana," she'd protest when her grandmother had her bow her head for grace. "Then pray for others," Nana Tempo would chide. That seemed too overwhelming. For what would Jackie plead—and for whom? World peace? An end to war? To sickness? To death? From a very young age, Jackie wasn't quite sure what she believed; all she knew for certain was that she should try to do some good.

Now, however, Jackie found herself praying with every fiber of her being—a wordless plea that coursed through her body.

Please.

From the corner of her eye, Jackie noticed that her book had begun to glow. There, in the middle of the scholar's table, the ancient tome took on an unnatural hue and soon became the brightest object in the darkened room. As the last of the muezzin's mournful call echoed above the now-silent city, Shahan joined the Tempos as they huddled over the book.

"This one needs attention, too," David said, and tapped his own book, twin to Jackie's text.

The great table groaned as if under a terrible burden; the two books slid together as if by a powerful magnetic pull. The patterns of their covers merged into a swirling, hypnotic pattern, faster and faster still, generating a tremendous heat and energy. The scholar and the time travelers jumped back as the pages of both books started to flip at the same frenzied pace until the pages seemed to blur.

Then all at once, the books lay open and still, edges of the papers touching. It appeared as though the books had melded together, though Jackie noticed a slight movement at the edges of the pages.

"There!" She pointed to a map that appeared, shimmering to the surface of the pages as if from a great distance below. The scholar and the time travelers held their collective breath as borders separating sea and land were slowly marked on the paper, and a red line appeared in the Middle East, snaking its way to northern

Africa, southern Europe, and then—almost leaping across to the book on the left—to North America.

"Yes, this is what we know of the Islamic world," mused Shahan as he stared at the book on the right, which contained the large map of Africa, the Mediterranean world, and the Middle East. Like a glowing dot-to-dot, sparkling points of light served to connect the red lines. "But what is this?" He traced the line westward to the northern United States.

David and Judith Tempo stared at the book in shock. Jackie caught her breath.

"It's … it's where we're from," she stammered.

"Look!" Shahan stepped back; the points of light glowed golden. He shifted his gaze to the more familiar, the book on the left. "Ah," he said, nodding. His brow smoothed.

"Well?" Judith prompted him gently.

"These are some of the main cities of Dar al-Islam," Shahan explained. "Look here—Mecca, naturally, the starting point—and Baghdad, where we are now, and Alexandria"—his finger swerved to northeastern Africa—"Timbuktu, and Cordoba." His finger moved west and north, a slight skip across the Mediterranean as he tapped the final destination in Moorish Spain. He looked up at them expectantly.

David Tempo raised a brow and crossed his arms. "Yes, we can see that."

Shahan straightened up and adjusted his turban. "Each of these destinations—these great cities—is a major center of scholarship. Each boasts major universities and vast palaces of learning, great libraries."

Jackie nodded. "We just learned about this in class," she said to her parents. "We had to follow the travels of Ibn Battuta." She looked down at the glowing map and shook her head at all the distance the itinerant scholar had covered in seventeen years.

Shahan frowned. "Ibn who?"

Professor Tempo shook his head. "Never mind," he said and smiled at Jackie. "Wrong time period."

Judith Tempo leaned in. "It looks like … the great libraries of the known world are all connected somehow," she half whispered.

With that, the books began to glow ever brighter, and the red line shooting westward across the Atlantic seemed to leap off the page. Shahan, Jackie, and her parents stepped back, shielding their eyes from the intensity of the glare. The room became stiflingly hot. Jackie held her breath: the red line connected to northeast America, along the seaboard, and … possibly to Arborville? Dizzied, she put a hand to her own hot brow, and something tugged at the very edge of her consciousness. Could there be a connection between these libraries and her very own, across time and space, at Arborville High School?

"Ow!" There was a great cry and a thump from behind the secret door. Jackie glanced at the white-hot books on the table and then up at her parents. Her mother shook her head. There was no time to do anything about them. Without a word, the small group turned to face the disruption, shielding the precious books with their backs.

The vizier burst in, holding the slave boy by the back of his neck, shaking him like a frightened kitten. He cast the boy off with a flick of his hand, and the child crouched in the corner, crying wordlessly, tears marking a frightened course down his face.

"The boy swore he saw Achmed put a potion in your tea!" He saw that the scholars had not touched a drop. "Perhaps I should make this child sip of it himself, and we shall see!"

Jackie leaped forward and took the boy in her arms, shaking with fear and anger at the vizier's rough handling of the child.

David Tempo put a hand on Jackie's shoulder, barely restraining his anger at the vizier. "Don't you touch that boy!"

"You dare to defy me? I've had enough of this nonsense! Guards!" the vizier called, his thin body trembling with a fury it could barely contain. Now the slave boy had gone marble-white with terror. Six guards burst into the room and awaited their orders. The vizier pointed at Jackie, who staggered back at the sheer force of his hatred.

The vizier ripped Jackie's turban off her head. The guards stepped back in shock as the long cloth unfurled to reveal her streaming, flaming hair. The men flinched and averted their eyes.

"Well?" the vizier shrieked at their hesitation. "Arrest that ... that wretched girl!"

Do not consider it proof just because it is written in books, for a liar who will deceive with his tongue will not hesitate to do the same with his pen.
—Maimonides

Chapter XX

The Great Lie

The Center of the Worldly Universe, 2586 CE

"A LITTLE MORE TO THE left ... That's it, right there ..." Devon sighed with a pleasure that rippled through his entire being. The attendant dug her fingers, insistent and warm, deep into the soles of his feet. Devon relaxed into his Throne of Light, and as each satisfied breath sent its brilliant beams farther into space, the crowd before him gasped. Lord Devon was all-seeing, all-knowing; Lord Devon was God, and as such he had the Seat of Supreme Power. The throne adjusted to his every mood and move, and now, as he relaxed under the skill of the attendant, the throne illuminated the entire Hall of Heroes.

Lord Devon was satisfied; the supplicants were optimistic. They waited patiently for the Bestower of All Knowledge to answer their prayers, which they knew he did when he was feeling generous. "May he live long and forever," they murmured to one another, mother to child, husband to wife, stranger to stranger. Some had come from quite far to the Center of the Worldly Universe, but theirs was a common bond: they were united under the banner of One World Order, and Devon's rule everlasting had kept the peace for centuries.

"May the blessings of Lord Devon be upon thee," they offered.

"And also on thee," came the response.

"May he live forever."

"Indeed he shall."

A haunting tune rippled through the thousand-strong assembly; they knew the words well, but the minstrel's story was a stark reminder of what could have been—if not for Lord Devon.

Many, many moons ago when the earth was snowed
Under with letters and fettered with shackles of learning,
And brother fought brother, and mother too
Over true wisdom and meaning.
Too much to read, too much to hear, too much to know
Except rage coursing through it all.

The young minstrel paused, his voice catching with the emotion that surged through the great hall. Devon leaned back even farther, a deep, dark contentment coursing through every inch of his being. He knew what would come next. The masses, in all their finery and in all their rags, all as one, together gathered their collective breath, quiet at first, and then finishing with a great, affirming roar:

Devon is Light, not Learning;
He's done away with our yearning.
Warriors, Farmers, we are all one.
Thank Devon, no more Learning to be done.

Devon smirked. *Okay, so it's definitely not the best poetry, but who would know?*

He had done away with the Intellectuals centuries ago, when he had assumed his rightful place as emperor of the planet.

"Get out of here," he said to the attendant, so softly that she alone could hear the words; the crowd saw only the paternal smile he bestowed upon her. She backed down from the dais hastily, fixing her gaze on the light that emanated from the Seat of Power. It was still brilliant; she was safe. One more bow, and she melted into the crowd.

Devon leaned back into the Throne of Light, sending deep beams into the cavernous Hall of Heroes. He exhaled with anticipation, allowing the adoration of the masses to crest over him, a surging wave of respect as they chanted the story of his epic journey to power.

As well they should. *The Doings of Devon* was the only piece the masses learned now, and it was a proud oral tradition, passed from one generation to another. *I did that,* thought Devon. No more books now, save ... a few. He patted two texts that he kept tucked in his silken robes. Every once in a while, he'd pull them out to keep the people quiet.

"Is this what you want?" he'd roar, holding aloft the Book of the Past, revealing war and famine and terror writhing on its pages, glowing with an evil intensity.

"Or this?" Then he'd hold up the Book of the Future: it was calm and bland, its pages serene as he riffled through them in front of the people. "I am the Path to All Knowing and Understanding! Look around you and ask: what has become of your ancestors? What will be for your children?"

And they would fall back, as the memories of the wars without end were still fresh and in very little need of recounting.

Devon thought then of what he had wrought since he had first appeared in the twenty-sixth century. Now he was fully armed with a lost formula from ancient Egypt, which the alchemist had revealed as the key to immortality. Achmed had informed him that Shahan had stumbled upon it while translating an ancient Egyptian work, and had spirited it away from the House of Wisdom.

Devon also had the Book of the Future, which Achmed had indicated was back in his own real time: the twenty-first century. How Achmed knew, Devon had no idea; nor did he care. In fact, it was the very book Jackie had checked out, disguised as a text on Baghdad's House of Wisdom. How fitting. Devon chuckled to himself: *Typical grad student,* he thought. *My nose is always in a book. Well, no more!* And his smile was chased away quickly by a cruel look as he thought back on the events that had followed.

With the potion and his books—the Book of the Past and the Book of the Future—he was now in a position, in the twenty-sixth century, to rule the world. And with the power to see even further into the future and use technology that had yet to be created, Devon had quickly amassed a fortune.

He first made his mark in the pharmaceutical industry, using his wily intelligence to work his way to the top. With full collaboration from the government, he fast-tracked drugs that were designed to ease the fears of the people, from anxious kindergartners to worried bankers. At the same time, Devon gained control of the media and built his case for these drugs—putting them on a par with vitamins, complete with RDA—recommended daily allowance—labels.

Excellent move, he congratulated himself as he gazed out into the crowd. He had seen this trend grow in the twenty-first century as parents and doctors gave atypical behavior all sorts of labels and prescribed pills, rather than undertaking the task of having children assume responsibility for their actions. It was much, much easier to take a pill than to confront and handle all sorts of behavior—from overeating to anxiety.

Thus it was that he had come up with three pills to usher people through the main stages of life. The fears of childhood, adulthood, and old age were handled with SweetTime, Strengthify, and Prolonging, respectively. *They worked well, too,* thought Devon as he grinned into the glassy eyes and vacant smiles of those who worshipped him.

Oh, there were a few holdouts, those who dared to challenge his growing power and refused to take their so-called vitamins.

He had known that would happen, and he handled it by labeling. First, he named social groups and made them real through repetition in the media—on shows, in "respectable" journals, on the radio. They were the Spirituals, the Intellectuals, the Scientists, the Manufacturers, the Warriors, and the Farmers. The Manufacturers were businesspeople and workers all lumped into one, and he quickly had them slandered for their greedy, capitalistic ways. With inflammatory rhetoric urging them on, mobs set upon this productive group, destroying factories and offices. Soon there was no industry, for anyone seeking to make a profit was targeted as a traitor to a peaceful world. One incentive was that Devon reallocated lands to the most ruthless of persecutors; this was their reward for violence.

Of course, not all gave in easily, least of all the Intellectuals. Still, Devon sneered to himself, they were an easier target than he had anticipated. Books were burned and files were erased as Devon questioned the validity of research, academic inquiry, and discussion and challenged what he called the "empty, unproductive waste of words."

Of course, among the Intellectuals were religious scholars, who questioned Devon's growing power. And naturally, they were unwilling to give up their years of scholarship, which took them, so they believed, to Truth. But he had them slowly eradicated; all such troublemakers were dosed with small pink pills that rendered them submissive. The most rebellious were given extra doses, and if they didn't wake up, well, that was their problem.

As additional insurance against insurrection, Devon pitted the great religions against one another, planting stories in the media. Christians against Muslims, Jews, Buddhists. Sikh warriors rallied in the Punjab; soon religious wars spread across the planet, and no one was safe except those who pledged their allegiance to the One World Order.

Books were burned. All communication was controlled by the One World Order, and teaching across all lands was abandoned as the people sought to survive.

Then Devon appeared in all places at once, his New Media controlling the channels, preaching calm and bestowing blessings on those who would follow him.

Ah … this was what he had always dreamed of. Total control. Total domination and free will—his, of course. He glanced at the masses below the dais. They could wait. Of course, they had no other choice. He shifted contentedly.

"Sire! O sire, wake up!" Two fat grubby hands grasped at his ankles, and Devon sat up sharply.

"Ohh …" A collective gasp of horror rippled through the crowd as the Throne of Light went dark, the shafts of light swallowed by the Seat of Power and by Devon's anger. The Hall of Heroes went dark as well, save for three strategically placed torches that burned steadily, revealing the fear of the masses. Lord Devon was not pleased.

A baby whimpered, its cries quickly muffled by a scared mother.

Devon stood up for the first time in a few hours. He rocked back on his heels, a bit unsteady, collected himself, and glared at the poor, sweating messenger who was groveling in the white silk rug at his feet.

"Get up, pig! You're ruining my carpet!" Devon snapped. The stout man drew himself up slowly, quivering like gelatin. The messenger tried to smooth his white linen tunic with little success; his hands were shaking too much to be of any use.

"Well—get on with it!" Devon pushed the little man hard, and he staggered backward.

The messenger blinked and recovered enough to deliver his message: "There's been a breach, sire—of s-s-security."

Devon froze at the words, shocked at the messenger's indiscretion. Whatever it was could be handled, but the messenger had spoken far too loudly—it would never do to have word of this breach get out. The illusion of total control had to be maintained at all costs. Devon shuddered to think of how the crowd would respond if they knew the truth. *I should have the fool executed,* he thought. Rage boiled up inside him, and he glanced at his praetorian guard, always at the ready to do his terrible bidding.

The messenger quickly collected himself and whispered, "The walls of the Sacred Library are disappearing—into thin air!"

I have read thy letter. Thou shalt not hear, thou shalt see my reply.
—Harun al-Rashid

Chapter XXI

Limbo

Between Worlds

JON WATCHED HIS FINGERS DISAPPEAR; curiously, he felt only a strange calm, nothing else. He put out his right leg and watched it fade to nothingness, too, and then suddenly, he was on the other side.

He glanced down at his feet. They weren't on any solid ground that he could see, but they were definitely on some kind of floor. He pushed his dark hair out of his eyes, sweating, and took a tentative step forward—into the bright, opaque nothingness.

"This is a dream," he whispered, but when he punched his thigh, he felt his body absorb the blow. "Or maybe I'm dead?" Then, a bit more loudly: "Uh—anyone out there? Anyone?" He couldn't see a thing. He walked blindly into the light, in no particular direction, arms bent at the elbows, hands up in a slightly defensive position.

As he inched his way forward, Jon thought about what was supposed to lie beyond mortal life. The extremes were either nothingness—or so believed the ancient Mesopotamians with their House of Darkness and Dust—or eternal freedom, should one break free from the cycle of reincarnation to reach nirvana, as the Buddhists claimed. He recalled a particularly heated exchange in his world history class, when Ms. Thompson had asked, "What happens to us when we die?"

Within a few minutes, the whole class was arguing about it. Just when the discussion seemed about to spiral out of control, the pretty teacher raised her hand: "We're all smart, thinking beings, right? So what accounts for all this anger?" They then went on to the discuss the European Holy Crusades, and how Muslims and Jews fought side by side against Christians in their Holy Lands.

Well, I guess I'm on a weird crusade of my own, Jon thought wryly. *On a mission to find Jackie. Not so very different from searching for the Holy Grail, in terms of difficulty—or at the very least making some sense of what the heck is going on.*

"That's it, over here." A man's voice, deep and rich, cut through the vast opaqueness, and then Jon could make out a lanky figure beckoning him forward. The space brightened and cleared, and now the man gestured to him to sit down. Two large leather armchairs were pulled together, separated by a mahogany side table, upon which a brass lamp cast a soft glow.

Jon moved forward and stepped onto a richly patterned burgundy carpet with a knotted ivory fringe. *Guess this is the border of the House of ... Nothingness,* he thought idly. He felt no fear. *The only way through is through,* he thought next, a phrase he'd repeat over and over during the toughest, most painful part of his cross-country races. But he was feeling no pain now, and he was compelled to move forward. Jon shook his head, dark hair tumbling over his brow.

The man indicated that he should sit, and he did, their knees almost touching. They were both tall, and each sank as far back into the plush chairs as possible. The man had a kind face and warm hazel eyes. He smiled gently at Jon, and Jon instinctively mirrored his expression.

"Wait a minute ..." Jon sat straight up. "I've seen you before!" He took in the man's salt-and-pepper hair, boyishly cut in prep school fashion, his affluent appearance. Now the man grinned, and reached into the right pocket of his brown corduroy pants to pull out a pipe.

"Have you, now? Well, I guess that's all right, then." He drew on his pipe and offered his right hand. "Allow me to introduce myself anyway, Mr. Durrie."

Jon started at the sound of his own name, but grasped the man's hand in a firm handshake.

"I'm Gordon Knotte." The man smiled at the bewildered teen.

"What?" Jon was stunned. "I thought you were dead!" He strained forward, his dark brows furrowed, diagonal slashes against his pale face. "You're not, are you—and neither am I, right?"

Gordon pointed just beyond the border of the rich carpet.

What had passed for ground fell away, and Jon could see his body, head cradled by his arms, slumped over a desk in the far corner of the Arborville High School library. His backpack was partially open, a mess of papers peeking over the top of the frayed fabric. This Jon's mouth was open, and he shut it, then, turning his head away from them.

"Was I just drooling?" The sentient Jon, in another time and space, was on his feet now. "God, how stupid!" He whirled on Gordon, who was standing as well, puffing calmly on his pipe. "What's going on? Is this a dream world?" Jon demanded, fists clenched.

"No, don't punch yourself again." Gordon grinned. They were about the same height, which Jon found a bit disconcerting, used as he was to hovering over everyone else. Gordon put a hand on his shoulder, and Jon was instantly flooded with calm as he stared into the man's deep hazel eyes.

"Awake or dreaming … I'm in the high school library … but where are you, then?" Jon continued to stare at the older man.

Gordon shook his head sadly. "We're in another … place, if that's the word for it." He pointed off into the distance, and Jon could see the town of Arborville, everyone going about their day. "Well, I suppose you could see … what you want to see."

Gordon glanced over Jon's shoulder, and both saw Jon's mother frowning at her computer screen. She looked particularly lovely, young and absorbed in thought. Then she scribbled something on the pad beside her computer and started typing again.

"Yes, I knew her ... before this ..." Gordon addressed Jon's unanswered question.

So Jon saw his mother hard at work on her novel, and his brother humming to himself as he marched along to his next class. He could see Aunt Isobel, folding embroidered swaths of silk in one of her vast storerooms. In the kitchen, Dona Marta was humming a popular Brazilian tune and peering into what appeared to be a bean stew. Wolfe paced through the great rooms of Shangri-la.

Jon could see all of this around him, even at his feet. *Like a helicopter ride,* he thought then, and he had a dim memory—or was it his imagination?—of taking off over a vast forest, and it seemed to him that he was in the whole world at once, even as the ground fell away beneath his feet. He shook his head, trying to clear the image.

"Here." Now Gordon gripped Jon's shoulder hard, steering him to an unpleasant scene.

He saw Jackie pushed up against a thick table, her right arm twisted behind her back so she couldn't move. Her auburn hair cascaded over her face, and he caught the terror in her eyes. A tall, thinly bearded man in robes was yelling at her as she stared ahead. A small group of what appeared to be Arab scholars watched, frozen. A little boy cowered in the corner, tears streaming down his face; they appeared to be in a library of sorts.

Jon started forward, trying to make sense of the scene. His first instinct, however, was to protect Jackie. She was a martial artist, and could handle herself well, but still—she was his girl. Jon clenched his fists again, every muscle in his body taut with anger.

"And here." Gordon turned the stunned teen around. Now Jon saw Devon, clad in richly decorated robes and standing on a futuristic dais before hundreds of supplicants. Devon was bent in a fury over a small, trembling man who threw up his hands to shield himself from Devon's ire. Odd lights cast an eerie glow on the cavernous hall, and Jon could see a throng of supplicants go rigid with bated breath.

Jon's head was spinning now. "What the—," he sputtered, dark blue eyes glazing over. It was all too much to take in.

"Right. You saw the past … but this is the future." Gordon's pipe had gone out. The man stared at the scenes that flicked before him. "Unless something's done about it." He removed the pipe from his mouth and stared dully at the cold ashes. "Right now, all we can do is watch."

Jon shrank back into his chair and stared at the chilling scenes that played out before him, his mind racing furiously. He remembered what his mother used to tell him as she worked out the plots of her novels: "For every problem, there is a solution. There's always a way out." He knew that the line was a metaphor for handling the challenges of life. Repeating that mantra, and confronting the thought that he had control over his life, had long helped him through the most difficult of situations. This included her illness and the days he fought to keep his small family together through those very hard times.

But this … His eyes dulled as he watched the past, the present, and the future unwind before him like an endless spool of film. What he saw next drove him to the edge of despair.

The most excellent Jihad is that for the conquest of self.
—al-Bukhari

Chapter XXII

Inner Fight

Baghdad, 927 CE

"No!" Jackie spat. She was spun around and thrown up against the heavy scholar's table, her right arm twisted behind her. She arched in pain, and clenched her left fist; then her martial arts training kicked in. She drove her left elbow into the guard's stomach and swung her fist backward and down for a groin punch. But as the guard crumpled to the floor, another picked her up and slammed her into a stack of books.

David and Judith were restrained by guards who held scimitars to their throats. The vizier had anticipated potential trouble from the traveling foreigners, whose faithless ways meant that they could not be completely trusted. David Tempo leaned forward, eyes wide with fury at the sight of his daughter tossed across the room like a rag doll. The veins in his neck strained as if they would burst, and a thin trickle of blood made its way down his neck from where he had leaned into the point of the blade in his anger.

"Now then," said the vizier calmly, clasping his hands in a pose of mock prayer, as if he'd just witnessed a silly schoolyard fight. He surveyed the scene before him: the two foreign scholars, terrible resentment sparking from their eyes; one of his guards staggering to his feet; and the redheaded girl attempting to do the same. He made a mental note to have the guard executed for his weakness. That the man was brought to his knees by a slight girl was ludicrous.

The vizier's small eyes narrowed, and his face tightened until it seemed that all one could see were his dark, bushy brows and scraggly beard. "Move!" he barked at the guards, and made his way to the table.

There, plain to see, were the two books fused together, swirling with a mysterious energy that was palpable to everyone in the room. The books glowed with a fierce intensity. Achmed burst into the room and pushed his way over to see for himself. His eyes narrowed, and his breath rasped loudly in the heavy silence. He reached for the books, but was pushed down by an invisible force. He adjusted his turban and staggered to his feet. "I have always loved a good fight," he muttered, an odd grin fixed to his sweating face.

The vizier cast him a strange look and then gestured to Jackie. "Go to them." He indicated the books. It was clear that no one else could touch them, and he was curious to see what would happen next.

Jackie tucked an auburn curl behind her small ear, squared her jaw, and straightened up. Her head was throbbing, but she would not reveal her pain in front of her parents, much less strangers. She would do the vizier's bidding, of course, but in her own good time. A smattering of small freckles stood out coldly against her pale face. She took a deep breath and stepped forward.

She felt like a pawn in the universe of life, small and pulled about by forces invisible. *A victim of the gods,* she thought, *moved about as they so please. A piece, moving forward, not of my own free will, but rather according to some master design ... created by someone else.*

But she could still respond with dignity; that much was in her control. She recalled Epictetus, the famous Stoic: "*Difficulties* are things that show a person what they are." Well, she—Jackie Tempo—had been through enough, but she could still be strong. She was little, yes, not physically big at all, but not to be trifled with. Pawn that she was, she was still her own unique piece. But one day, soon, she would control how she moved about the board, this game of life.

And thus it was that Jackie set her jaw and tamped down her fears. The pain in her back and the throbbing at her temple spiraled beneath her consciousness, and from somewhere deep within, she felt a source of energy and light, coursing through her body like a river in the spring. She was alive; she had free will within this strange universe.

Judith took a sharp breath and reached for David's hand. Their daughter's natural beauty took on an unearthly radiance as she did the vizier's bidding.

Jackie reached for the books, her unbound silken hair a red veil that swung forward and obscured the ancient texts. Suddenly the room took on an unearthly hue, and Jackie's face shone in the unnatural light. She was lifted slightly off the ground by a strange energy that coiled itself around her and left her smiling, breathless and warm. Red motes of dust surrounded her, swirling and sparking, fiery flakes, shielding her from all the pain in the room. She tossed her head back and laughed now, shaking out her long red curls and exposing her creamy throat, and she threw up her arms for sheer joy, palms up, the mysterious dust swirling through her fingers, pooling in the cup of her palms.

"*Ai!* Have mercy!" A scimitar clattered to the ground as a guard prostrated himself on the cold floor. The other guards followed suit. David and Judith had drawn closer together in awe, and the little slave boy stared up in wonder, tears dried on his cheeks, eyes round and shiny as newly minted dinars. Shahan stood stock-still, taking it all in, his scholar's mind racing, calculating … It couldn't be.

"You!" exclaimed the vizier, furious and shaken. His world was falling to pieces. The room filled with a roar, the sound of an ocean, and the vizier raised his voice to speak above the din.

He jabbed a bony finger at Shahan. "Tell me everything! What ... what is that!"

Words failed Shahan, so he pointed to the robes piled next to the vizier, where Achmed had stood just moments ago. Then Shahan glanced up at Jackie, still suspended in the air. As they watched, she was set gently down. The sparkling dust coursed around her once again, then shot straight up to the ceiling and disappeared.

Shahan swallowed hard and cleared his throat. It seemed to him that his voice came from far, far away—from another time and place. But he was conscious that his feet were planted firmly on the ground, and held fast to that awareness. He glanced at Jackie, embraced now by more earthly beings—her parents.

"That was ..." He looked at Jackie with wonder. "That was her jinni."

Jackie rubbed her eyes; this was all too much to take in.

"Impossible!" David Tempo shook his head, arm firmly about his daughter's shoulders. "Genies are a myth."

Shahan shook his head. "And her jinni is now doing battle." He pointed at Achmed's robes again. "Achmed is not of our world," he said. "He is, in fact, also a jinni, and can thus assume any form he so desires. So your daughter's jinni has disappeared—to do battle." Shahan closed his eyes at the thought. "I should have known."

"But—to do battle with whom? Or what?" David Tempo drew his small family close.

"Her jinni is in a fight to the death with what we perceived as Achmed, clearly a most evil, malicious jinni, a maelstrom of hell, a spiteful force that has caused much of all that has ever gone wrong in the history of this world." He paused, and looked about the stunned group. Shahan was known for the breadth of his studies; young though he was, he was quite serious. The guards sat back on their heels and looked up expectantly.

"I suggest that you pray." Shahan's eyes were as dark as the terrible fear in his heart. "All of our fates depend on the outcome."

He who indulges in falsehood will find the paths of paradise shut to him.
—Abu Bakr

Chapter XXIII

A Pure Heart

The Center of the Worldly Universe, 2586 CE

"Guards!" Achmed called out with imperial authority. He had not failed in his promise to Devon. As the façade of complete authority began to give way when the messenger blurted out the bad news, Devon had tapped his staff three times on the dais. Achmed appeared within seconds, ready to confront any challenge to his master.

The tall, burly men on either side of the heavy, iron-hinged wooden door snapped to attention and crossed their pikes to block entrance to the forbidden room. Their dark eyes, visible through the designs of their gleaming helmets, shone with a deadly menace. These men were part of the most martial militia on the planet, trained to kill since childhood. As such, they relished the most deadly of challenges.

The men refused to move at first; one had raised his hand in a threat to the insolent speaker. But when they saw the elite entourage behind Achmed, they uncrossed their pikes and dropped to one knee.

"Lord," they said in unison. Devon swept by the guards and patted one on the helmet.

"That's right," he responded, sailing past the men to push open the heavy door. He flung his silken cape over his shoulder and wrinkled his nose.

The windowless room gave off a faint, rotting scent, and as Devon stepped across the threshold, a tired-looking old man got to his feet. He had been sitting at a lone wooden table in front of a small pile of books.

"Sire." The man bowed, drawing his loose robes in as he did so. He was a small, thin man with a faint wisp of a white beard. He closed his eyes as he bent his head, and his face, worn by the ravages of time, looked as if it might dissolve to dust at any moment.

"So what did you need to show us?" Devon had stopped just over the threshold, wrinkling his nose once more at the stale odor.

Achmed, on the other hand, brushed right past him into the tiny room. "Begging your forgiveness, sire," he said, nodding to Devon. Then he frowned at the old man, who seemed to shrink further into his dirty robe. "Speak, Director!"

The library director, reminded of his position of authority— such as it was—drew himself up to his full stature, which reached only to Achmed's shoulder. Still, in doing so, he displayed a vestige of his former self.

"As director of Baghdad's House of Wisdom," he said coldly, "and now … this"—he spat, waving his hand dismissively at the small pile of books—"it is my moral duty to report on any concerns regarding the safekeeping of the manuscripts in our … library." The director bit off the last word with palpable distaste.

Achmed sneered. "Remember your place, my director. You do not wield much power here. Your 'House of Wisdom' has … shrunk somewhat."

It was true. All the director controlled was this tiny room and a few books, a far cry from his duties more than a thousand years ago. Back in Baghdad, many centuries ago, the library director had been stunned by poison, and had appeared dead to the entire world. Devon had no trouble escorting him into the future. The man closed his eyes at the thought of all the learning that had been lost—on his watch.

He well remembered the day the stranger Devon had entered the House of Wisdom. The slight, pale man seemed lost and not a little uncomfortable in his scholarly robes. As was the custom, the director had excused himself from his research to greet the visitor and offer him such assistance as was needed. After all, the library was a palace of learning, and true knowledge could be obtained only with an open mind and heart, and painstaking dedication to the pursuit of Truth. Thus it was that scholars from Dar al-Islam and beyond were welcomed for their own—and sometimes peculiar—learning; the director well knew that there was truth in all honest learning, however strange it might be. This is why he agonized over the finer aspects of Euclidian geometry. There were answers—and truth and beauty—in every angle. "For every problem, there is a solution," he'd mumble under his breath, for this was what his own tutor had drummed into him from a young age. He'd used that thinking even beyond the academic world, repeating those words to his own wives, children, and grandchildren, and was well regarded in his own family and in the larger community as a gentle man of sound advice who always found solutions. Sometimes, though, the problems were quite difficult and the solutions hard to find. This was one such time. The director closed his eyes. Perhaps if he were more devout …

"*Merciful Allah*," the director prayed silently, "*thy will be done*." The mysteries of the Divine were indeed hidden to him. He had no idea how he had ended up in this small, mean universe with only a few books and almost no company. All he could do was watch, and pray, and keep his heart and mind open.

"Well, Mohammed?" Devon barked. "Out with it!"

A richly patterned curtain hung from the ceiling to the floor, just behind the wooden table, and Mohammed, the library director, lifted it now.

The small group dropped back at what they saw, gasping. Devon's face drained of color, and one of the guards fell to his knees.

"We are doomed," he wailed, hands clutching at his head. "Our world is ending!"

Devon pushed the guard over. "Shut up, you child," he snarled. "Perhaps you need to start taking more vitamins." The man whimpered and fell silent.

For the first time in a long, long while, the director felt the faintest stirrings of hope as he gazed at the frightened faces of the evil men before him. *Praise Allah,* he thought, *there might be a solution after all.* He could not even begin to explain it, but it was possible. Fascinated, he turned to the scene that had reduced the powerful men to quavering children.

There were no walls beyond the curtain. No windows or doors either, but a flicker of orange that crackled in the dingy room. A faint scent of sandalwood wafted over the group, and Mohammed, with nothing to lose, leaned in toward the shimmering border to another world.

That was, in fact, an unnecessary gesture, as the border actually shifted toward him. Mohammed could feel the heat of the shimmering wall as it advanced inch by inch until it fairly danced in front of his face. A few of his beard hairs sparked, singed down to the quick. Still, he did not move.

"Look!" shouted one of the guards, his deep voice tremulous with fear.

Just beyond the curtain, they could make out two swirling figures locked in what appeared to be a deadly struggle, one dark and the other golden bright.

The dark being rose up and up as far as the eye could see, and then came down fast and hard onto the light, which shattered in a million pieces. The men in the room shielded their eyes from the intensity of the glare. Then the light gathered up into a glowing golden orb and smothered the dark. The small library shuddered, and revealed hairline fractures from ceiling to floor. A thin cloud of dust covered the watching men.

"What …," Devon sputtered, wiping his mouth with the silken sleeve of his tunic, "what is this?" A deep, cold fear shot through him; his world was crumbling. He didn't even try to pretend to be royal anymore; he just wanted to survive.

"A battle of the jinnis," said Mohammed. "I should have known." He smiled to himself. "Now it all makes sense." He pointed to where Achmed had been just moments before. Here, too, all that now remained were his robes in an untidy heap by Devon's ankles.

Devon jumped. "What the—"

Mohammed, the library director of the House of Wisdom, smiled. "Now you know. Achmed was a jinni, able to assume a human form and obey your every desire, real or imagined, spoken or thought." He pointed to the swirling darkness. "There he is, battling a jinni for the good."

Then Mohammed turned his face full to the violent scene before him, eyes wide open. He was confronting the very essence of Truth itself and wanted to see it all. His eyes teared from the heat of the shimmering wall, which advanced on him with every second. He was ready; his heart was pure.

It is better to sit alone than in company with the bad;
and it is better still to sit with the good than alone.
It is better to speak to a seeker of knowledge than to remain silent;
but silence is better than idle words.
—al-Bukhari

Chapter XXIV

Falling

Between Worlds

Jon felt a rumbling at his feet, and the heavy armchairs shifted slightly. He caught the floor lamp just before it crashed to the ground.

"Nice save." Slightly out of breath, Gordon nodded to the athletic young man.

"What's going on?" Jon stepped to the edge of the fringed Persian carpet and was instantly thrown back by a tremendous force. The agile teen righted himself and bent his knees for balance as he rode the powerful surge. Gordon crouched next to him, and together they peered over the edge of the silken rug.

There below, and suddenly up and all around them, were two swirling figures, one sparkling red, the other an inky black, dervishes locked in a mighty struggle. They stretched far and wide, filling up the view. The ground buckled again, but still the men kept to their feet, watchful and not a little anxious.

Jon started to sweat from the intense heat the beings generated, and he noticed Gordon wiping his brow as well. A great roar filled their ears, and it seemed that the end of the world had come. But Jon could see through the locked beings to Jackie, unmoving, in a frozen tableau with two people who appeared to be her parents. Somewhere in the future, Jon could see Devon as well, mouth agape, an unspoken horror reflected in his eyes. He could see his mother, frowning at her computer screen, and then Aunt Isobel, who paused in the act of folding her kimono collection. She glanced up, hesitant, humming a tuneless song. What did they all see?

But he had eyes, really, only for Jackie, her red hair swirling all around her pale face. Jon was tired of being left behind, or in the way. He had had enough. His chest ached—with fear or longing, he couldn't tell. But as surely as he knew that he existed, and that time ticked on, he knew he needed to be there, right next to her—his rightful place.

"Go to her." Gordon knew exactly what he was thinking. "At least one of us can leave if we try hard enough." Then he shoved Jon over the tasseled borders of the rich Persian rug and back into Jackie's life.

We come spinning out of nothingness, scattering stars like dust.
—Rumi

Chapter XXV

Then—and Now

Baghdad, 927 CE

A THOUSAND SPARKS, AND AN endless roar, filling her ears with the solid sands of time. Buried, where she had once been. Nothing else. Jackie bent her arms, palms up and out, as if to ward off the inevitable: her erasure—and the disappearance of them all. She never would have been. *They* never would have been.

Then Jon, gripping her hand, tightly mooring her to the present. Back in the now. The dull roar receded, and the room cleared as the last motes climbed up the wary light of the flickering candles.

The Center of the Worldly Universe, 2586 CE

"Noooo ...!" Devon screamed and tore at his robes, flailing madly. His guards backed out the door, aghast at the scene. The room was disintegrating around him, and he was spinning in an opaque half-light, clutching at space. Everyone fell away, and the last thing he saw before he was slammed into unconsciousness was Mohammed's wide grin.

"Thy will be done."

Between Worlds

"Well, I'll be damned." Gordon settled back into his chair and relit his pipe. He glanced up at the scenes that played out before him, one after another, in rapid succession: He saw Aunt Isobel lift her head from *The Tales of the Genji*; Wolfe, curled up beside her on the library couch, opened an eye and yawned. "Silly old dog," she said fondly, and scratched the top of his head. He saw Jon's mother lean back from her computer, eyes filled with tears. She had finished her novel. And he saw Mrs. Housel, switching on the library lights, greeting the first class of the day. She was smiling broadly. From the far corner of the library, Jon shook himself awake and passed a hand over his face. How long had he been out?

"Until we meet again," Gordon said, and Jon looked up sharply. Then the high school senior stuffed his notes back into his book bag and strode out purposefully. He was looking for Jackie.

When I want to understand what is happening today or try to
decide what will happen tomorrow, I look back.
–Omar Khayyam

Chapter XXVI

The Way Back Home

Baghdad, 927 CE

THE VIZIER COLLECTED HIMSELF, DREW a shaky breath, and turned to Shahan. "I thought I had asked you for an explanation."

Shahan shook his head and blinked, as if awakening from a deep slumber. "Now I understand." He rubbed his eyes and stared at the small group, who looked back at him blankly. He noticed that the young man beside Jackie had vanished.

"Each of the four books from Samarkand is the vessel of a jinni—that is, a powerful spirit that can assume human or animal form." Shahan spoke slowly, allowing the group time to absorb the meaning of his words. The little slave boy brightened at the thought of a magical being in their midst; Judith reached for her husband's hand.

"So the jinni belongs to whoever releases him—it—from the vessel," the young scholar continued with a nod to Judith, "and so it is that you and your sister, Isobel, share the spirit of your book. You did, after all, open it together, is that correct?"

Judith reached for her copy on the table and caressed its swirling designs. Then she clasped it against her heart. "Yes," she whispered. "And we have traveled far together."

The vizier rocked back on his heels, eyes narrowed, stroking his thin beard. "I thought jinnis had free will."

"They do—to a point," explained Shahan. "The Qur'an references the power of these sentient beings, but they are, in fact, quite loyal. They like to anticipate and indulge their masters' thoughts."

Jackie tilted her head. "So maybe that explains Aunt Isobel's travels …" She caught her mother's eye. "And your own ability to track Devon through time."

"Right, and your own path, as well, always back to us." Judith and David pulled their daughter into a warm embrace. "Strange that they have not revealed themselves to us."

"Oh, but they have … through your thoughts and desires. Whoever awakens, or ignites, the book first basically imprints the jinni with their thoughts, and that can include the desire to share the book's—or rather, the jinni's—power with another."

"So that's why my husband and I have both used our book and are always reunited?" asked Judith.

"Yes. You are pulled toward each other, and that has always been so," answered Shahan, and none in the room could fail to note the look of tenderness that passed between husband and wife.

Jackie spoke up. "And that's why it's possible that my aunt Isobel and I might share our book, the one I found in her library?"

Shahan nodded. "Yes, your aunt might have wished for you to seek out your parents, when the time was right." He looked at the group. "But note: jinnis don't always take on a physical form, unless it's absolutely necessary." He paused, furrowing his young brow. "But this Devon has awakened a powerful, evil force that has, in fact, corrupted his soul. This force was on a quest for total domination and immortality, and it wanted to be seen. And since jinnis can assume human or animal form, we can, in fact, make an educated guess about the identity of this jinni among us."

They all glanced at the robe and turban on the floor, where Achmed had once been.

"Achmed." A whistling sound escaped from the vizier's lips.

"Right," said Shahan. "This jinni—'Achmed'—led the foreigner Devon to the fourth book, with its own mysterious power, and it is this which has catapulted him to the future, where he is living out his most base desires."

"Not anymore." A small figure emerged from the shadows. He was grinning broadly, arms wide to greet the group.

The slave boy jumped up and gladly wrapped his arms around the man's torso, a big smile to match the man's own.

"Director! You've come back!" the little boy cried with relief.

The library director threw back his head and laughed. "Yes, dear boy, I've come back." The kindly man hugged the boy. "And I have seen that you, my son, have done well." Mohammed's dark eyes twinkled with knowing. "I know you can read—in several different languages. You know that you can rise above your slave status, as have I, to serve in the House of Wisdom!" He stood up, and the boy held his hand in a tight grip of gladness.

He locked eyes with the vizier. "He is gone," said Mohammed, the softness of his voice tinged with anger. "Praise be Allah, the man is gone."

Jackie furrowed her brow. "But where?"

The director started at the sight of an unveiled woman in their midst. He glanced at the vizier, who held his tongue. "To another time, surely," he answered, looking away from the heathen sight. "He has not finished with his journey, although his travels to the future are now over." Mohammed held a small, cold book in his hands. It was the same size and heft as the others from Samarkand, adorned with arabesque, but unlike the others, it was titled: *Infinite Knowledge, Eternal Life: The House of Wisdom.*

Jackie drew a sharp breath. "That's the book I—" The director held up a hand, and it was as if he could read her mind.

"All libraries—Houses of Wisdom—are connected by virtue of their ability to transport their patrons to other times and places through the many doors each book represents. You could almost say every book has a special jinni for each of its readers, as every book has the potential to touch its readers' very souls and alter the course of their lives. But this is a mystery, and where the reader goes is not for another to discuss. Please, say no more."

Jackie nodded.

"Good," said the director. "So it is best that the book remain where the truest of scholars may attempt to understand it. I believe this book should stay here." He looked at Jackie Tempo and her parents, and then gave a gentle smile. "Unlike the three of you."

"But first we must dine, my friend," said the vizier, clapping a hand on the old man's shoulder. "Have we forgotten our roots, the Bedouin tradition of hospitality?" He smiled at Shahan and the Tempos. "Umm al-Muqtadir and her qahramana are most interested in our red-haired guest." He nodded at Jackie. "And she holds her foreign 'friend' hostage for now. I say we return to share the tale, for I have learned not only that it is prudent to be in the good graces of the caliph's mother but that she is certain to feed us all well!" He was in a generous mood; a major catastrophe had been deterred, and he wanted to make up for his earlier tirade. He patted the little boy's head. "I am sure you may sup with us as well, as Umm al-Muqtadir has a soft spot for talented children." The boy's face lit up.

Jackie laughed, and her parents gave her a querying look. "I would not cross her, that's for sure." Suddenly she realized she was starving. She threw her erstwhile turban over her hair in an attempt at a hijab, and the little boy giggled at her clumsy efforts.

"No? Well, how's this? Or how about ..." And thus it was that the House of Wisdom, so often alive with intense academic discussion, was brightened by lively peals of laughter as Jackie grinned and tried to make herself presentable.

* * *

Dinner was even more lively as the unlikely group gathered together to share Umm al-Muqtadir's hospitality. The caliph's mother joined in the meal, clearly in high spirits, ready for a good story from her guests. But first she shared her own good news: it pleased her no end to make a substantial financial contribution for the creation of a charity house for poor women and their children on the outskirts of Baghdad.

"For what sort of Muslim woman should I be if I did not donate alms to the poor?" This was to be her third such project, and she was energized. Jackie marveled at the woman's high color, and could see that she had once been quite beautiful indeed.

"Indeed, charity is a pillar of Islam, and you have upheld it well, my lady," murmured the vizier.

The caliph's mother shot him a sidelong glance and a sly smile. "I am quite charitable—and merciful," she replied, and Shahan was seized by a short coughing fit. There was no one in Baghdad who hadn't heard of the vizier's earlier run-in with the powerful Umm al-Muqtadir.

Meanwhile, Anthony had fallen into deep conversation with Shahan and the library director.

"You actually have ancient manuscripts, like from ancient Greece, right here in your library? How do you know they're real? And who do you let actually touch them?" Jackie had never seen Anthony so uninhibited and genuinely interested in anything before; he looked like a young boy, eyes sparkling, trying hard not to interrupt the scholars with his questions.

She sat quietly with her parents, basking in the glow of their love. For the moment, they were all able to pretend they were a solid family unit again.

David Tempo put on a mock stern face. "So tell me about your grades, young lady. You had better be earning straight As in history."

Jackie gave her dad a slight push. "Now I am, ever since Aunt Isobel introduced me to Jon …" Her voice trailed off.

Her parents exchanged glances. "He seems very special to you," Judith said softly, stroking her daughter's cheek. "We're glad you've made friends in Arborville." She glanced at Anthony.

"Yes, I have," Jackie replied, and put her hands in her lap. She had lost her appetite. "I wish you could meet them," she said, head down. But she knew the answer. One day, they would, in fact, be reunited for good. For now, however, a terrible crisis had been averted, and that had to be enough. Devon was someplace else in time, and still had the potential to cause a fair amount of trouble. But he no longer had the immediate power to directly dictate the future—and thus erase the past.

* * *

Jackie and Anthony walked away from the lively laughter, toward the main door that led out of the room, making their way to a keyhole arch. He thought they were merely going out into the courtyard for a breath of fresh air. But she knew better. This was their way back home.

"You know, you were right before," he said. "I was going to quit AP World History because my friends—former friends—made fun of me. They said I wasn't man enough to hang out with them anymore." He fell silent, not wishing to reveal the totality of their taunting. "But basically, I've just got to *man* up and deal with them."

"Right," Jackie said quietly. "You have to follow your own path, and it might often be lonely."

"Aw, dude, I'm sorry," Anthony said, patting her shoulder awkwardly. "I'm such a jerk, thinking about my own issues." He paused just before they went through the luminescent arch, an entry, she knew from past experience, into another world—her own. She had learned that when the time was right, a door would present itself and she would walk back into her own time. "Well, as long as you have good friends—and you know you've got me—you can get through anything, right?"

Jackie nodded. She swallowed hard, choking down the pain of tears held back. She knew she was lucky for being so loved by her parents and Aunt Isobel, and for having such great friends in Anthony and Jon. But she was walking away from her family once again. Not forever, she knew now.

And so they moved through the portal and were stunned by the brightness of the stars that lit up the evening sky. Anthony whistled as he stared up. Indeed, the sight was spectacular. Jackie squinted up at the display, dazzled by the light, and locked her left arm in his. She clutched her book from Samarkand in her right hand, and as she did so, an incredible, nurturing warmth surrounded her, and she felt at peace. *Maybe that's my jinni?* she wondered, giving herself over to a most pleasant, drifting sensation. She tripped into the courtyard with Anthony and put her hand out for protection. He held it, tight.

"Jackie? What's happening to us—" She heard his voice as if from very great distance, and then she heard no more. Then she was falling, falling, falling, and she closed her eyes to prevent a rising tide of nausea. Finally she gave herself over to having no control at all as she tumbled into space.

An insistent bell clanged for what seemed to be an eternity. She was jostled—by Anthony?—and opened her eyes.

Arborville High School, present time

"Jackie?"

Jon reached out to touch her shoulder, and she lifted her face to his in a deep smile as students milled all about them. Through the glass doors, Mrs. Housel caught Jackie's eye and gave a short wave, and then turned to Anthony with a surprised look. Jackie smiled as the librarian and her former problem student began an earnest conversation about research.

Jon pulled her out the library door.

"School's out. You really need to leave this place," he said. He meant the library. "C'mon, you need to get a life!"

"Like Anthony?" They could see Mrs. Housel pointing excitedly at a certain section in the stacks. Anthony seemed intrigued, and he put his backpack down on a nearby table. *He* was obviously staying to work on their project.

"All right, let's get out of here and go someplace ... fun." Jackie laughed and held his hand.

"Another adventure?" Jon smiled down at her. "I'm sure that can be arranged."

THE END

Works Consulted

El-Cheik, Nadia Ma. "The Qahramâna in the Abbasid Court: Position and Functions." *Studia Islamica* 97 (2003): 41–55. Print.

———. "Revisiting the Abbasid Harems." *Journal of Middle East Women's Studies* 1.3 (2005): 1–19. Print.

Lewis, Bernard. *The Muslim Discovery of Europe.* New York: Norton, 2001. Print.

Mackensen, Ruth Stellhorn. "Four Great Libraries of Medieval Baghdad." *The Library Quarterly* 2.3 (1932): 279–99. Print.

Marlow Taylor, Gail. "The Book of Secrets: Alchemy and the Laboratory Manual from Al-Razi to Libavius, 920–1597 C.E.." *World History Bulletin* XXV.2 (2009): 11–18. Print.

Tignor, Robert L. *Worlds Together, Worlds Apart: A History of the World from the Beginnings of Humankind to the Present.* New York: Norton, 2008. Print.

"Umm Al-Muqtadir-Billah." *WISE Muslim Women.* Web. 04 Aug. 2011. http://www.wisemuslimwomen.org/muslimwomen/bio/umm_al-muqtadir-billah/.

En los últimos años ha aumentado la literatura sobre la catolicidad de la iglesia. Todas las iglesias la reivindican en cierta medida. La Iglesia católica romana hace un gran trabajo al presentarse a sí misma como la verdadera iglesia "católica", haciendo que los protestantes se sientan como si la hubieran abandonado o hubieran roto con ella. Este serio estudio de Andrés Messmer hace la afirmación contraria, i.e., la catolicidad de Roma es más romana que "católica" y hay un sentido en el que el protestantismo histórico es el heredero de la catolicidad bíblica y las tradiciones de manera mucho más profundo que Roma. Messmer ofrece un argumento convincente y erudito y, al hacerlo, brinda una magnífica oportunidad para que protestantes evangélicos y católicos romanos entablen un dialogo profundo sobre lo que significa defender la catolicidad de la Iglesia en nuestra generación. Han pasado muchos años desde que John Henry Newman dijera que "profundizar en la historia es dejar de ser protestante". Sencillamente es insostenible. El estudio de Messmer argumenta de manera concluyente que el protestantismo es "católico" pero no romano y que la Iglesia católica romana tiene un serio problema teológico al querer mezclar sus pretensiones de ser "católica" y su romano centrismo.

Leonardo de Chirico,
Reformanda Initiative (Roma, Italia).

El profesor Messmer argumenta persuasivamente que todos los evangélicos debemos darnos cuenta de la diferencia entre la catolicidad genuina y el catolicismo romano para reclamar nuestra identidad católica y fortalecer nuestro testimonio común del Evangelio. Su libro explica claramente esta importante diferencia y defiende con firmeza lo que él describe como catolicidad reformada.

Daniel Eguiluz, misionero y profesor,
Serge Global (Lima, Perú).